"Sometimes the answer is right there in front of you."

"You're right, Addie." Dev caught her wrist as he rose from the stool. "Sometimes it is. All you have to do is look. I've been looking for a long, long time. And look what I've found."

He released her wrist to raise his hand to her hair. He'd been wanting—waiting for a lifetime—to pull those clips and bands from the top of her head, to watch the sunshine-bright strands fall around her shoulders, to plunge his hands into her thick, luscious hair. And now she was here, standing before him with her eyes wide and locked on his and her lips parted in a breathless surprise that matched his own.

Her lids fluttered closed as his thigh brushed hers. "I don't know what you want from me."

"Yes, you do. We could start with a kiss and go from there."

"A kiss?"

"Do you need a demonstration?"

She huffed out a shaky little breath and opened her eyes, tilting back her head to give him a sassy smirk. "I know what a kiss is."

"Yes, but you've never been kissed by me."

Dear Reader,

When people ask me what I do for a living, I tell them I write love stories for Harlequin. I always enjoy seeing their faces light up at my response—at the idea of having a justifiable excuse to spend lots of time in my own make-believe worlds with characters whose struggles always end happily. Writing—and reading—love stories is a terrific way to spend the day, don't you think?

In *A Small-Town Reunion,* I enjoyed creating a world in which a first love gets a second chance. And I got the opportunity to experiment with a craft I'd always wanted to learn: making stained glass windows. You see, I had one of those justifiable reasons to satisfy my curiosity: the heroine in this book is a stained-glass artist. Sometimes I not only create interesting careers and adventures for my characters—I get to share in a bit of them, too.

I always love to hear from my readers! Please come for a visit to my Web site at www.terrymclaughlin.com, or find me at wetnoodleposse.blogspot.com or www.superauthors.com, or write to me at PO Box 5838, Eureka, CA 95502.

Wishing you stories with happy endings,

Terry McLaughlin

A Small-Town Reunion
Terry McLaughlin

HARLEQUIN®

TORONTO • NEW YORK • LONDON
AMSTERDAM • PARIS • SYDNEY • HAMBURG
STOCKHOLM • ATHENS • TOKYO • MILAN • MADRID
PRAGUE • WARSAW • BUDAPEST • AUCKLAND

Recycling programs
for this product may
not exist in your area.

ISBN-13: 978-0-373-71605-0

A SMALL-TOWN REUNION

Copyright © 2009 by Teresa A. McLaughlin.

ABOUT THE AUTHOR

Terry McLaughlin spent a dozen years teaching a variety of subjects including anthropology, music appreciation, English, drafting, drama and history to a variety of students from kindergarten to college before she discovered romance novels and fell in love with love stories. When she's not reading and writing, she enjoys traveling and planning house and garden improvement projects. Terry lives with her husband in Northern California on a tiny ranch in the redwoods. Visit her at www.terrymclaughlin.com.

Books by Terry McLaughlin

For Rick at The Glass Works with gratitude for his patience with all my questions and for the stained-glass beauty he's added to our home.

CHAPTER ONE

AN EXPLOSION JOLTED Addie Sutton awake to a shuddering, dark world of groaning woodwork and rattling windowpanes. Her bedroom floor jerked and pitched in nauseating waves, and her tall oak dresser pitched forward and slammed against the iron frame at the foot of her bed.

Not an explosion.

An earthquake.

"Dilly!" She grabbed her oversize cat before he could leap from his spot beside her. A dresser drawer jounced open, wedging against her foot and spewing socks and lingerie over the quilt. The lamp on her nightstand toppled and smashed on the wood floor. Shards from the Tiffany-style shade skittered and danced across the hardwood planks, spreading in a path that threatened to shred bare feet and paws.

She clasped the hissing, struggling cat to her chest, shrinking against her pillows to wait it out. For how long—twenty seconds? Thirty? How strong were the tremors? Where was the epicenter? It could be anywhere—this stretch of the northern California coast was a crazy quilt of fault lines.

Another crack-and-jerk rammed the headboard against the folding screen behind it, toppling the divider separating her sleeping alcove from the living area of her small apartment. Somewhere in the kitchen something fell and shattered. How much more broken glass would she find in her shop?

"The shop," she whispered in the sudden silence marking the end of the final tremor.

A Slice of Light—her stained glass shop in Carnelian Cove. She stared at the jagged, moonlit pieces on her floor and wondered if she'd find more costly rubble scattered about the workplace beyond her apartment door. She had to get out there, to check on her projects and supplies, to try to salvage and stow what she could before the aftershocks hit.

With a quake that strong, aftershocks were sure to follow.

She kicked free of the quilt, slid across the mattress and carried Dilly to the armoire angled in one corner of her bedroom space. She managed to keep her grip on her squirming pet while she slipped into a pair of flip-flops, and then she dumped him into the cramped closet area.

"Sorry, Dill," she said as she shut the door. "You may develop a case of kitty claustrophobia, but it's better than slicing up your paws."

She shoved the dresser upright with a grunt, then carefully picked her way around the remains of the lamp shade. Edging past the fallen screen and into the open living space, she flipped the switch for the chandelier swaying above her kitchen table. *"Oh, no."*

The pretty little pitcher she'd stuffed with marguerites the evening before had broken in a dozen pieces when it hit the floor. Books had slumped and slid from their shelves, and two of them lay facedown in the puddle of flower-specked water. She plucked them from the wet mess and mopped at the pages with a corner of the tablecloth before spreading them open to dry.

Behind her, the cell phone on her nightstand trilled an inappropriately cheerful tune. She lifted the screen as she moved toward her bedroom area, folding it so it would stand upright and out of the way. Soft light from the chandelier fell across the face of the old enamel clock hanging on the wall opposite her bed, and she squinted to make out the time. Five forty-three. It would be light soon; sunrise came early in late June.

She picked up the phone and returned to the kitchen. "Hello?"

"Addie." Lena Sutton, her mother, had always been able to inject galaxies of worry and relief—or impatience and annoyance—into that one word. "Are you all right?"

"Yeah, I'm okay." Addie rolled her tiny island butcher block back into place and frowned at the remains of a fruit bowl at her feet. "I've found a broken lamp and a vase and bowl so far, but I managed to catch Dilly before he stepped on the pieces. How about you?"

"I'm fine. Just a few things to set right, a few pictures to straighten. Goodness, I'm still shaking," her mother added with a short, breathy laugh. "That was a wild one."

"It sure was." Addie stared at the indistinct outline of her reception counter through the lacy folds of the curtains in the windows that divided her apartment from her business. "I'm almost afraid to look in the shop."

"All that glass." Lena heaved one of her I-knew-there-would-be-trouble sighs. "Call me right back, as soon as you've checked things out."

"There's probably no cause for alarm. And if there is, it might take a while to assess the damage."

Addie swept aside one of the panels of lace and peered into the darkened shop. Shadows angled across the storage shelves and flowed over the floor, cloaking the evidence. If she found too much breakage, she didn't know what she'd do—she couldn't afford to replace ruined stock, and she couldn't afford a hike in her insurance rates.

She grabbed the hem of her nightshirt and twisted the fabric in her fist. "I'd better get out there and have a look. I've got to open in a few hours."

"That's right. You're busy." Lena's tone had shifted into a familiar gear: politely strained and faintly injured. "Sorry I bothered you. I won't keep you, then. I just wanted to make sure you were all right."

"I told you—I'm fine." Addie pressed two fingers against the spot between her eyes, where a headache brewed. Sometimes it was difficult to be patient with her mother, but Addie always dug deep to find the appreciation she deserved. Addie had never known her father—he'd disappeared shortly after Lena had informed him she was pregnant. Her mother had sacrificed so much to give her daughter everything she needed; surely Addie could afford to spare her a little time. "And it's not a bother," she added. "Thank you for checking up on me. I appreciate it, really."

"I know you do. You're a good girl, Addie."

"Yep, that's me," she agreed with a weak smile. "A good girl."

She disconnected and stood for a short while as pearly dawn light tickled its way through a fuzzy blanket of fog. *A good girl.* A twenty-nine-year-old wimp with an overweight cat, an overbearing mother and a business teetering on the brink of bankruptcy.

A faint rumble shot her pulse into triple digits before she identified the sound as a passing fire truck— probably an earthquake-related emergency call. She straightened, sucked in a deep breath and aimed her attitude toward positive as she pulled her broom from the cupboard. It was just another Thursday, and she had a new day to face and responsibilities to handle. But first, she had a cat to rescue.

BY OPENING TIME, Addie had cleared the mess in her shop and was beginning to inventory the full extent of the damage. An entire section of rough-rolled and glue-chip glass was gone, and the sample box of cathedral-glass squares had fallen from its shelf, damaging the tiled tabletop below. She'd called her insurance agent to discuss the possibility of a claim, and she'd fretted over how she'd deal with the deductible.

Her lips thinned in a tight, tense frown as she swept shards too small to use for scrap into her dustpan. A Slice of Light's financial situation was so precarious that one good shove would send it toppling over the edge. She hoped this earthquake hadn't been the shove to do it.

"Morning." Tess Roussel, the Cove's newest architect and one of Addie's best friends, strode into the shop on a pair of stylish heels, wearing a neon-pink sundress and toting a matching neon-pink handbag and two cups of takeout coffees from the café around the corner. "I wanted to see if you'd survived. Hell of a way to start a Thursday."

"I'm all right," Addie said as she took one of the cups. The rich, earthy scent of the brew triggered a rumble through her empty midsection, reminding her she'd skipped breakfast. "I'm not so sure about Dilly. He's probably considering running away from home."

"That tubbo tabby?" Tess brushed polished fingertips through her short, black hair. "He'd never make it past his food bowl."

Sipping her coffee, Tess wandered to the deep storage bins suspended on one of the brick side walls, noting the empty spaces. "I see all the reds are gone. And most of the yellows, too."

"Figures the most expensive stock would be the stuff to fall." Addie dumped the contents of the dustpan into her industrial-size trash bin. "I don't know how I'm going to replace it."

"You've got to replace it. We need it for Tidewaters."

Tidewaters was Tess's masterpiece, a clever combination of fabulous commercial space and gorgeous condo units under construction along the waterfront. She'd generously incorporated several stained-glass windows and panels into her design, and Addie had counted on that upcoming contract to give her business a needed boost.

"Believe me, I'm aware of that," Addie said. "That project is the one thing that's keeping me from advertising a going-out-of-business sale."

"You can't quit. And it's not just because I need you." Tess gestured toward the fanciful displays hanging in the window. "You've poured everything you've got into this business. Besides, you're too talented to simply give up and walk away from it."

"Thanks for the support. You have no idea how much it means to me." Addie shoved the broom into its cupboard. "But talent doesn't pay the bills. I haven't sold anything in days. Summer's always tough without the university students around to shop for their projects, but I can usually count on the tourists to fill in the gap. This year the gap's gotten wider. Lately the window-shoppers haven't been buying any windows."

"What about your idea for classes?" Tess rested her hip against the corner of a display table, letting one of her long legs dangle. "With the delays at Tidewaters, you could squeeze some in before business picks up again."

Addie winced at Tess's mention of the setbacks at the construction site. A stretch of vandalism had ended two weeks earlier in a spectacular blaze, leveling the framed skeleton of Tess's design to its foundation. Tess had been devastated, but she'd rebounded almost immediately with a surprising engagement to Quinn, the general contractor on the project. Now the two of them were working harder than ever to raise their building from the ashes.

"I can't just advertise classes," Addie said. "I need to come up with lesson plans, and check on the insurance, and—"

"So do it." Tess took another sip of her coffee. "And get a move on. Offer a special summer session for whiny ten-year-olds, and I promise Rosie Quinn will be the first to sign up."

"You want me to offer a bunch of kids the opportunity to slice themselves on cut glass or burn themselves with soldering irons?"

"So it wasn't one of my most brilliant ideas." Tess shrugged. "Desperation must be taking its toll."

Addie smiled. It was a struggle imagining her friend as a stepmother—and Addie was certain Tess was having the same trouble adjusting to the idea. "Is Rosie giving you trouble?"

"Nothing I can't handle with tranquilizers and pain relievers. For me, not the kid," Tess added. "I'm sure we'll figure things out, right about the time she leaves for college."

"What about kids of your own?"

"God." Tess grimaced and lowered her cup. "Let's talk about something more pleasant, like a nuclear blast on Main Street. Or how we're going to get Charlie to commit to a date for her bridal shower."

"I'm relieved she finally set a date for the wedding." Charlie Keene, their friend since elementary-school days, had agreed to marry Jack Maguire, her new business partner in Keene Concrete. But Charlie's dread of being the center of public attention and her dislike of formal social events, shopping, lace and tulle were complicating the wedding plans.

And Tess's love of the social events and shopping Charlie detested—not to mention her fondness for organizing her friends' personal business—had made her the logical choice for Charlie's maid of honor.

"Jack threatened to arrange for a flock of doves and a dance orchestra," Tess said. "That got her minimalist rear in gear."

"Even his threats are romantic," Addie said with a dreamy sigh. "He really loves her, doesn't he?"

"Poor guy." Tess grinned. "I remember threatening

him with thumbscrews when he first blew into town. Turns out getting engaged to Charlie was worse than any torture I could have dreamed up."

Addie slid onto one of the work stools behind her long reception counter. "They're going to be very happy together."

"Yeah, they deserve each other, all right. And don't get your feathers ruffled," Tess added when she caught Addie's frown. "I mean that in the nicest possible way."

Tess dropped her empty cup in the giant bin as she headed toward the door. "Better swing by my office before I head out to check up on Quinn and give him his midmorning kiss."

"That's so sweet." Addie's smile was wide and guileless. "He deserves you, too."

Tess paused, her hand on the doorknob and her eyes narrowed in suspicion. "Sometimes I think that syrupy sweet exterior of yours is a fiendishly clever disguise. Beneath all that fluffy gold hair, those big blue eyes and those angelic dimples lurks the heart of a serial insulter."

"You know I always try to avoid hurting anyone's feelings."

"Like I said," Tess added as she headed out the door, "fiendishly clever."

Addie watched her friend climb into her bright red roadster and speed off toward the waterfront. Tess had Quinn; Charlie had Jack. Currently, Addie had Mick O'Shaughnessy, a baseball-playing carpenter on Quinn's construction crew—though she wasn't quite sure what to do with him. Their relationship seemed to be skidding from romantic to platonic.

Addie also had bridesmaid duties to perform and

bills to pay. She switched on her aging disk player, popped in a CD of Motown classics and reached for her sketches for a new set of window ornaments.

Five minutes later, the sun had burned through the morning fog to fire summer light into every corner of the shop, and a honeymooning couple had wandered in to admire a hummingbird and rose done in filmy opalescent and clear textured glasses. She excused herself when her desk phone rang.

"A Slice of Light, Addie Sutton speaking."

"Hello, Addie."

She stiffened. It had been several years since she'd heard Geneva Chandler's voice on the phone. "Good morning, Mrs. Chandler."

"Must we be so formal?" Geneva, Tessa's grandmother and the wealthiest woman in Carnelian Cove, had once employed Addie's mother as housekeeper. Addie had lived most of her childhood at Chandler House, playing quietly in a corner of the enormous kitchen or tucked up in her attic bedroom.

Or romping in Tess's suite, when her friend had come north to visit. Tess had grown up in San Francisco, but she'd spent school holidays and long summers in Carnelian Cove. Geneva had often claimed the two of them were a matched set, like night and day.

"Formal?" Addie twirled a strand of hair around a finger so tightly her knuckle turned white. "No, I don't suppose so. What can I do for you, Geneva?"

"Two of my windows were damaged last night during the quake. I'd like you to come out today and see about repairing them for me."

"Which ones?"

"Two of the set over the entry stair landing. You know the group."

"Yes, I do."

Addie had spent dozens of hours nestled in one corner of that landing, her picture books propped on her bony knees and her toes digging into the thick, richly patterned carpet, while rainbows flooded through the glass to drench her in color. She'd studied the intricate webbing of lead, had observed the infinite effects created by sunlight as it played through the waves and streaks and bevels. She'd told herself stories to bring the patterns and pictures to life as they'd painted her skin in jeweled tones and pastels.

Those windows had been her secret, silent joy. They'd kept her company and given shape to her dreams—and now two of them had been broken. It was as though pieces of her childhood had been chipped and fractured.

"Can you come?" asked Geneva. "This morning, if possible. I'd like to get an expert opinion on how to proceed with the repairs. And, of course, I'd like you to make those repairs for me, Addie."

"Yes, I'll come." Of course she would. Her special, magic windows needed her skills.

And Addie had always known there'd come a day she'd be forced to deal with the Chandlers.

HALF AN HOUR BEFORE she'd agreed to meet Geneva at Chandler House, Addie stared at the mirror hanging above her bathroom's wall-mounted sink and tugged her fingers through her long, curling hair. It was a simple matter of basic grooming and good manners, she reasoned as she twisted together a few tendrils and caught them up with two tiny, spangled shooting-star clips. Looking put together on the outside would help her feel put together on the inside—even if the butterfly horde in her stomach was flapping hard enough to propel a space shuttle into orbit.

She wasn't trying to impress Geneva, she told herself as she slipped thin gold hoops through her ears. Even if she'd wanted to, it was impossible to impress a woman who had more power than anyone else in town. The Chandlers had made their fortune in the timber industry and then earned several more through marriages to heiresses and investments in a number of Carnelian Cove businesses. There were few citizens of Carnelian Cove who hadn't benefited, directly or indirectly, from the family's employment opportunities or charity projects.

Addie smoothed a hand over her powder-blue short-sleeved shirt and stared at the toes peeking through the ends of her sandals, wondering if another layer of lotion would pass for a pedicure, and then decided her canvas deck shoes were more appropriate for the visit.

Her old truck sputtered and shuddered as she backed out of her alley parking spot, and its idle seemed rougher than usual as she waited to pull on to Main Street. Time for another tune-up, she thought with a sigh—and where was she going to find the cash for that?

From her bill for the repair on Geneva's windows, she realized. She'd ask for a deposit and use some of the funds to replace her broken supplies. Chances were she'd need those supplies to make the repairs, anyway.

Sunlight pierced the shadows beneath the bluff's redwood grove and flashed across the windshield as her truck groaned and complained about the climb up the winding road. She passed the crooked, scarred rhododendron that Tess at sixteen had swiped with her new roadster and remembered the way she'd screamed as the shredded purple blooms exploded in their faces. There was the turn to Danny Silva's house—the infamous scene of the poolside party where Addie had lost her bathing suit top after a clumsy dive.

And there, near the top of the bluff, was the entrance to the Chandler estate. It seemed days rather than years since she'd driven through these tall, wide, iron gates. Nothing had changed—the flowers and ferns spilling over the edges of fat stone urns, the lawn flowing like an emerald river from the slate-edged porches of the shingle-style house, the dramatic backdrop of tall trees and black cliffs.

No, she thought again as she tickled her clutch through a downshift—there was one thing here that had changed. She had changed. She was no longer the daughter of the housekeeper; she was an independent businesswoman here on a job.

She slowed as she neared a fork in the drive. One paved path led to the front of the house, swinging past the grand front porch before it curved beneath a porte cochere at the side. The other veered toward the rear, widening to form a courtyard connecting the service entrance with a separate two-story garage building. Surrendering to sentimental habit, Addie pulled to a stop near the kitchen door.

She climbed the concrete steps and hesitated at the narrow landing. She'd never before knocked on this door; her mother or Julia had always been on the other side.

Julia was still here, Addie knew, well into her sixties and as territorial as ever. It was nearly impossible to imagine the Chandler House kitchen without Julia in command, waving one of her wooden spoons like a baton to emphasize whatever point she was making. Geneva's cook had seemed ancient to Addie when she'd first seen her that afternoon more than twenty-four years past. Lena had plopped her five-year-old daughter on one of the kitchen stools, handed her a box of worn crayons and a few scraps of paper and warned her to stay out of the cook's way.

Addie had lowered her head, terrified of the sour-faced, wire-haired woman who shuffled around the room, banging her wicked-looking utensils against her shiny copper pots and muttering in her scratchy, booming voice. Eventually, Addie grabbed her very best pink crayon for security, escaping into a fantasy world of fluffy clouds and ponies and castles. A few minutes later, a plate of sugar-coated cookies slid into view across the wide central island, and Julia had asked her to draw a picture of a fairy princess with a crown of stars. In pink, of course.

Addie checked her star-shaped hair clips and smoothed a hand over her wrinkled shirt. She'd spent a sizeable chunk of thirteen years in Julia's kitchen, from shortly after her fifth birthday until she was ready for college at eighteen. Would Julia be here this morning? Certainly someone would hear the bell, Addie told herself as she pressed the small button centered in a shiny, ornate brass plate.

A few seconds later, the dark green door swung open to reveal a tall, lean man with long, bare feet, a white shirt hanging unbuttoned over a pair of ragged jeans, shower-dampened black hair, a half-eaten piece of toast slathered with jam and a wicked smile.

A man who had her smothering a startled cry and feeling as though she were missing vital pieces of her wardrobe along with every bit of her composure. A man who'd always been able to make her feel small and out of place. A man who'd also been the subject of most of her preteen daydreams and starred in far too many of her adult fantasies.

Devlin Chandler.

CHAPTER TWO

FOR A MOMENT ADDIE FORGOT why she had come to Chandler House. And why she could never, ever think of something to say to Dev to get past him and over him and forget him and move on with her life. *Because he's Dev Chandler, and he's simply the most beautiful man you've ever met.* Look at him, standing there the way he is, acting as if he owns the world—or all the best parts of it, anyway.

And in the next instant Addie reminded herself that she *had* forgotten him, and that she'd made an excellent start on getting over him. That she was here because his grandmother had asked her to come—because she had talents and abilities and had made a damn good life for herself.

But she still had to get past him.

"Who is it?" boomed a familiar voice from the kitchen.

Dev's mouth curved at one corner with one of his devil's spawn half grins. "Good question."

Julia shoved him aside with a muttered curse, and then her homely face creased in a wide, long-toothed grin when she saw Addie. "If it isn't Miss Addie. Come in, come in. Just look at you, so neat and trim in your pretty summer things. If you aren't a sight for sore eyes. And it just so happens I've got some of your favorite cookies sitting in my jar, just waiting for you to finish them up."

She latched on to Addie's arm with one of her knobby-fingered hands and tugged her inside. The scents of cinnamon and nutmeg rode on the thick, warm kitchen air, but Addie's skin prickled with the icy awareness of Dev's stare.

"You settle yourself on that stool, right there," Julia insisted, "just like old times, and I'll pour us both a cup of hot tea. And you can tell me what you've been up to."

"Go ahead," said Dev as he tossed his unfinished toast into the sink. "Don't mind me. I can get my own tea and cookies."

"That's right," said Julia with a wink for Addie. "We won't mind you one bit. And you keep your sneaky mitts off those cookies."

"The cookies sound great," Addie remarked. "But I'm not here to visit. I have an appointment with Mrs. Chandler."

Julia turned with a frown, the plate of cookies in her hand. "Did you say 'Mrs. Chandler'?"

"I'm here on business," Addie said. "To take a look at the damage to some windows."

Dev nipped the plate from Julia's hand. "I'll take those."

Julia snatched them back with a scowl. "You'll take Addie to find Geneva, is what you'll do. Now get out of my kitchen. You've been pestering me all morning, keeping me from getting my work done."

Dev darted to the side and stole a cookie. "I've been keeping you company, you old windbag."

Julia pulled the towel from her shoulder with a practiced move and snapped it at Dev's arm.

"*Ow.*" The cookie fell to the floor.

"Is Geneva in her office?" Addie asked.

Dev began to button his shirt. "I'll take you."

"You don't have to. I'll just—"

"I said I'd take you." He unfastened the top snap on his jeans and stuffed his shirt into his waistband. Behind his back, Julia rolled her eyes and muttered something about manners.

"If she's not in her office," he said, ignoring the cook, "what are you going to do—hunt all over this place for her?"

Addie crossed her arms. "I thought I'd start by checking out the windows." She glanced at his bare feet. "I take it the area has been cleared of any broken glass?"

"Nope." He shot her another crooked grin. "We thought we'd leave that to the expert. *Ow,*" he said again as he darted out of towel range.

"When you're finished upstairs," Julia told Addie, "you come right back here. I want to hear all your news."

Addie followed Dev through the sunny breakfast nook and cavernous dining room toward the marble-floored foyer. She caught a glimpse of new wallcovering in one room and reupholstered chairs in another, but everything else was as it had always been. The scents in the formal parts of the house were the same, too—citrus polish, lavender water, old books and wool carpets.

And then there was Dev. The same wide shoulders set in a perpetual slouch, the same slightly wavy hair in need of a trim, the same casual gait stuck somewhere between a shuffle and a swagger. The heir apparent of Chandler House; the only son of Geneva's only son. She wondered why he was here, how long he'd stay, whether he was married—no, he wasn't married. She was sure she'd have heard the news from Tess, his cousin.

But why hadn't Tess mentioned he was back in town?

Addie slowed and paused when they reached the grand entry to the front parlor, staring up at the set of stained-glass windows depicting the four seasons. She couldn't see any damage from this angle; maybe things weren't as bad as she'd feared.

Dev stopped, too, and when she finally lowered her gaze from the glass, she found him watching her.

"What have you been up to, anyway?" he asked.

"Wh-what do you mean?"

"Are you married? Divorced?"

For one second, a ridiculous wave of joy rushed through her at the fact that he seemed interested enough to ask, to make an attempt to start a conversation with her. And in the next instant, her pitiful little thrill whirled down the drain as she realized he didn't know the most basic facts about her—and that he'd never cared enough to find out.

"I beg your pardon?" she asked.

He frowned and shoved his hands into his pockets. "Never mind."

"No, I—" She shook her head, knocked off balance by her over-the-top reaction and his serious expression. "No, I'm not married."

He waited, as if he expected her to say something

else. His dark-eyed gaze roamed over her features, assessing, testing. And then the corner of his mouth tipped up in one of his cocky grins. "Go on up to your windows, if you want to," he said with a jerk of his chin toward the stairway. "I'll tell Geneva you're here."

DEV SOFTLY KNOCKED on one of the tall, paneled pocket doors leading to the old smoking library his grandmother used for her private office and waited for her invitation to enter. Instead, one of the doors slid aside on silent casters. "Is Addie here?" asked Geneva.

"She's in the entry, waiting for you." He turned to head back to the kitchen.

"Wait."

Geneva angled through the narrow opening, commanding her pack of whiny, yappy little Yorkies to sit and stay behind. She wore casual, caramel-colored slacks and a sporty linen top on her tall, amazingly youthful frame. But the pearls at her ears and the elegant twist of her upswept gray hair reminded him she was a no-nonsense woman who expected proper behavior in all things, at all times. "I'd like you to hear what she has to say," she said.

As he followed his grandmother back toward the entry hall, he wondered what the old lady was up to. She was up to something—Geneva's demands were never eccentric and sometimes Machiavellian. He didn't like being caught like a cog in her current machinations, but he didn't know how to avoid it as long as he was taking advantage of her hospitality.

And he'd continue to take advantage of the situation because he was up to something, too. Several somethings, he mused as Geneva greeted her beautiful—and single—stained-glass specialist. For the time being, he was content to remain exactly where he was, following his grandmother's lead.

Trailing after the ladies provided an unexpected bonus. At about eye level, Addie's shapely butt swayed back and forth as she climbed to the landing between the first and second floors. *Nice.* She'd always been a looker—and it seemed he'd always been looking in her direction. Hard to avoid it, with her attending the same schools and spending so much time in the same house. No point in avoiding it, not when the looking was such a pleasure.

And Dev had never seen the point in avoiding pleasure.

He'd done his best to avoid Addie, though. At first it had been easy—she was just a kid, three years younger and a useless female. A timid little thing with big, watchful eyes, a golden-haired mouse who'd scurry out of his way whenever he entered a room. He'd been confused and lonely after his parents had divorced, lonelier still after his father had wrangled custody from his mother and then left him, for the most part, in Geneva's strict care.

So Dev had vented his frustrations on the naive girl who was his most convenient target. Even if he hadn't already ruined the possibility of a friendship with his bullying, he'd never have lowered himself to seek the companionship of a shy, dreamy kid who spent her time drawing pictures.

Beautiful pictures. Fanciful, dreamlike scenes. Yes, he'd done his best to avoid her, but he'd been smitten with her all the same.

And years later, after he'd discovered females

weren't entirely worthless, he'd realized Addie had more to offer than most of them. Her dreaminess had blossomed into a creativity that intrigued him. And her shyness had transformed into a calming presence that attracted him with its promise of peace.

But there'd been no point in making a bigger mess of his life than necessary. Geneva had warned him about putting the moves on the housekeeper's daughter, and Addie's mother had given him a silent version of the same message. Addie herself had flashed the hands-off signal like a neon skyscraper on the Vegas strip. This morning's chilly exchange had let him know nothing had changed.

Nothing but the passage of twelve years since his high school graduation, a mouth-watering deepening of her sexy voice and a refinement of the padding on those interesting feminine curves. And his own deepened and refined appreciation for both her curves and her attitude.

He frowned as he remembered that awkward pause earlier when he'd opened the kitchen service door and they'd stood there, staring at each other like a couple of dumbstruck kids. She'd looked at him as if she'd expected him to slip a snake into her pocket or trip her as she walked up the steps. And he'd wondered how her expression would have changed if she'd known his thoughts involved something scarier than a slithery reptile and just as likely to knock her off balance.

Now she dropped to her knees beside the damaged windows and plucked a few bits of glass from the carpet runner. "Is this everything that came loose?"

"No. Most of it's outside, on the ground beneath the foundation shrubs." Geneva clasped her hands at her

waist. "I wasn't sure whether you'd need those fragments, so I left everything as I found it."

"How did this happen?" Addie peered more closely
at the long crack in a wavy yellow panel. Beside that
piece, dented metal framework outlined empty spaces.
"Stained-glass windows are usually sturdier than others."

"One of the statues on the upper level fell from its
pedestal. The tremors must have sent it rolling down
the stairs, and it crashed against the glass, as you see."

Addie ran her fingers over a section of damaged
lead. "How old are these windows?"

"My husband had them installed when the house
was built, shortly before he and I were married. So
they're at least fifty years old."

"I'll take a look at the exteriors to see if there's any
sign of deterioration." Addie leaned in closer to the
glass. "I don't see any signs of bowing, so it might be
another twenty or thirty years before they need
complete reconstruction."

"Reconstruction?"

"You're close to the ocean here. Salt in the air can
cause the lead to deteriorate over time."

Addie frowned as she studied the windows. "I'm
not going to be able to simply patch these up, you
know. I'll match the missing pieces as well as I can,
but they may not be exactly the same. A lot of this is
high-quality antique glass, and suitable replacements
are going to be hard to track down."

"I'm sure whatever you can manage will be acceptable."

"I'm sure you'll be pleased with whatever I
'manage.'" Addie wiped her hands on her jeans as she
stood, and then she leveled a bland look at Geneva.

"And whatever that is, I assure you it will be a great deal more than acceptable."

Geneva gave her a tight smile. "Very well, then. When can you start?"

"Once I find the glass I need and order it. This weekend, perhaps. More likely the week or two after that."

"Sooner would be better."

"I'm sure it would."

Dev smiled at the subtle clash of wills, grateful his grandmother had insisted he stick around for the show.

"Well?" asked Geneva, raising one eyebrow. "Will it be sooner, then?"

"I'll need to arrange for some help getting these windows removed."

"You need to take the entire window?" Geneva stroked a hand over a curve of ruby-red glass. "Can't you fix them here?"

"Not without setting up a duplicate shop." Addie trailed her fingers along a twisting length of lead, her gesture resembled Geneva's. "And even then, I'd still have to remove the windows from their frames."

"Then take them." Geneva inhaled deeply and squared her shoulders. "Do what you need to do. As quickly as possible. Devlin will help you."

"I need expert help," Addie clarified, ignoring Geneva's suggestions and his presence. "And I'll need crates made to brace and transport them. I'll call Quinn to come and take a look at what needs to be done."

Geneva hesitated and then nodded. "All right. I'll have Devlin arrange for Quinn to meet you here, and then the men can get the windows out of the wall and into their crates."

Addie narrowed her eyes. "Quinn and I can take care of everything."

"I'm sure the windows must be quite heavy," said Geneva. "Quinn will need Devlin's help."

"If he needs any help," said Addie, "he can—"

"Don't bother checking with me." Dev crossed his arms and leaned against a newel post. "Just pretend I'm not here, that I have nothing better to do while you two make your plans."

Though she didn't move so much as an eyelash in his direction, the flare of pink in Addie's cheeks told him she'd noted the tone beneath his remark.

"When I need your input, Devlin, I'll ask for it." Geneva turned and started down the stairs. "Addie, you can use the phone in my office to make your call."

Addie stared at Geneva's back until the elderly woman stepped onto the marble foyer floor and disappeared around a corner. And then she shifted to face him, her expression completely shuttered, those wide, sapphire-blue eyes of hers devoid of the slightest hint of emotion or reaction as they settled on his.

And then, for just one second—for a slice of time as narrow and fragile and sharp as one of the slivers of glass—she let him in. And on that lovely face of hers— a face that had slipped through his memories and drifted through his dreams—he could read the evidence of one more thing that hadn't changed with the passage of all the years. She'd hidden it well enough throughout the morning's appointment, but in that instant he could see it in every line of her ramrod-straight posture and in every puff of the icy vapor that emanated from her frosty exterior: Addie Sutton's deep and abiding contempt.

ADDIE HAD LEARNED a long time ago to surrender to her mother's wishes when she didn't have the energy, or time to spare, for a siege. So when Lena had called with a dinner invitation that afternoon, Addie had postponed plans with her friends and agreed to travel across town to the riverside apartment complex her mother managed in exchange for her rent. The rest of the bills got paid with the money she earned cleaning offices after hours.

Her mother had once dreamed of a house of her own, Addie recalled, as she parked her truck in a guest spot in the complex's lot. A house with a yard for a swingset and a place where Addie could leave her toys and crayons strewn about if she chose. But Lena hadn't possessed any special skills or education, and the housekeeping job at Chandler House came with room and board, and a welcome for her daughter.

After a time, Lena had begun night classes, studying to be a bookkeeper. She'd demonstrated a talent for spreadsheets, and when she'd graduated from the course during Addie's sophomore year in high school, Geneva's son Jonah, had given her a job in his office downtown. A good job with the area's most important businessman. An opportunity to leave Chandler House, to renew her earlier dream of saving for a place of her own.

But that dream had died three years later, shortly before Addie's graduation. Jonah's car had gone off a winding cliffside road. And in the days that followed, Lena had discovered sixty-two thousand dollars was missing from the business account—a sum she'd been accused of embezzling.

She hadn't been guilty; Geneva Chandler had

agreed, refusing to press charges. But the mystery of the missing funds had never been solved. And Lena had never again found employment as a bookkeeper, not after such a big scandal in such a small town.

Lena opened the ground-floor door and pulled Addie into a quick, tight hug. "I know you're busy, and I know I'm being a pest, but I had to see for myself that you came through that quake all right."

"I told you on the phone," Addie said as she eased out of her mother's arms, "everything's fine."

"You said some of your shop glass was broken." Lena took the pink Bern's Bakery box Addie handed her and carried it into her compact kitchen. "Did you file an insurance claim?"

"I found another way to replace the supplies."

Addie took her usual spot at the tidy table set for two. Her mother had folded her faded cotton-print napkins into the foiled stained-glass rings Addie had made for a birthday present years ago. Addie ran a fingertip over one of the pretty bevels. "I went to Chandler House today."

"Oh?"

Lena could pack a sky-high load of meaning into that one syllable. Tonight, disapproval underlined her stone-faced delivery.

Addie searched, as she so often did, for traces of herself in her mother's features. When she was younger, Addie had imagined she could find her father in the differences. But she'd soon abandoned that game, once she'd figured out she'd probably never see the man. It seemed fitting to give up on him, since he'd never given her or her mother anything. No contact, no assistance. Lena had never told her daughter who he was—not so much as his first name—and Addie had long ago ceased to care.

She could see her own saturated blue in her mother's eyes and a bright hint of gold twining through the older woman's darker hair. But Lena's face was thinner, her cheeks less curvy and her jaw less sculptured. It was as though age and hard times and bitterness had worn her features.

Addie lowered her eyes, guilty over her unkind thoughts. "Two of the stained-glass windows were broken," she stated. "Do you remember the set on the landing between the main floor and the bedroom floor?"

"The four seasons. Yes, I remember." Lena ladled seafood chowder into a large bowl. "I'm sorry to hear it."

"She's hired me to fix them."

"I suppose that means you'll be spending a lot of time at the house."

"As little as possible." Addie pulled her napkin from its glass ring as Lena set the bowl of soup in front of her. "I've already had the windows removed and delivered to my shop."

Lena took her own seat without comment.

"She sent a 'hello' for you," Addie said.

"Who did?"

"Geneva."

"Oh."

Addie cut off a sigh and leaned forward, hoping her mother would raise her eyes to meet her gaze. "She asked how you were."

Lena idly stirred her thick soup. "That was kind of her."

"She'd be more than kind to you if you'd give her the chance."

"I don't want Geneva's charity." Lena lifted a basket of rolls and handed it to Addie. "Or her pity, or anything else she'd care to offer."

"I was talking about friendship."

"We were never friends." Lena shredded one of the rolls on her plate. "We were friendly. There's a difference."

"I don't think Geneva ever saw it that way."

"She wasn't your employer."

"She is now."

It wasn't often that Addie disagreed with her mother. The silences that stretched through the tense times that followed their arguments weren't worth the trouble. Jonah Chandler was dead; Geneva Chandler had become the focus of Lena's bitterness and resentment.

Addie sought a new topic, but the only thing that came to mind wasn't a subject she particularly cared to discuss. "Did you know Dev was back?"

"No." Lena paused with a spoonful of soup near her mouth. "And even if I had known, it doesn't matter," she said with a meaningful glance.

Addie was tempted to confess that it did matter. He still had an effect on her that she couldn't control. But she knew her outburst would be followed by a lecture instead of sympathy. Lena had a lecture for every situation concerning the Cove's most influential family.

And all those lectures ended with one essential piece of advice: never get involved with a Chandler.

CHAPTER THREE

ADDIE PULLED INTO Charlie's drive on Friday evening and parked behind Tess's sporty car. She jumped from her truck, exercised her temper by slamming the door and marched along the short walk to the front porch.

"Hi, Addie." Rosie Quinn, the daughter of Tess's fiancé, held one end of a chew rope. Charlie's naughty black Labrador retriever, Hardy, growled and tugged at the other end.

"Hi, Rosie. Staying for dinner?"

"Yep. Tess said we could have a girls' night." Rosie didn't bother to hide her delight at being included. "She brought a wedding video."

"Does Charlie know?"

"Not yet." Rosie worked the rope loose and tossed it across the yard for Hardy to chase. "Tess said we'd get some wine into her before we tie her to her sofa and make her watch."

Addie stepped up to the trim front porch and whacked the iron knocker hard against its panel on the Craftsmen-era door. Jack Maguire, Charlie's handsome fiancé, swung the door open. "Hey, Addie," he said with his Carolina drawl and megawatt smile. "Glad to see you're all in one piece."

It was hard to resist Jack's grin, especially when it

deepened those grooves on either side of his mouth. His dark blond hair was still damp from a recent shower, and he smelled of a spicy aftershave. His dark blue eyes crinkled at the corners as he looked her up and down, making a show of checking for earthquake damage.

Addie dredged up a strained smile of her own. "Thanks. I'm fine."

"If you say so." He stepped aside to let her in. "Charlie's back in the kitchen, watching Tess spoil a perfectly good rock cod with a mess of fancy fixings."

He trailed her through the house, and she noted his influence in the bright new paint on the wall behind Charlie's dull brown sofa and the glossy new finish on her secondhand dining-room table.

Addie halted in the kitchen doorway, her hands on her hips, and her eyes narrowed to slits as she glared at her so-called friends. "Why didn't one of you warn me Dev Chandler was back in town?"

"Because the earthquake sort of knocked that little detail from my mind." Tess, seated at the kitchen table, sliced through a lemon and picked out a seed. "And because I didn't think it was that big a deal."

"Well, it's not," Addie said.

"Could have fooled me." Charlie rinsed her hands at the farmhouse sink. Her thick, curly hair had been tamed in a braid hanging between her shoulders, but coppery tendrils escaped to twist and curl at her temples and nape. "Especially since you're standing there looking like you can't decide whether to kill us or yourself."

Addie tossed up her hands as she moved into the kitchen. "Okay, so I'm upset. Mostly I'm upset that I'm upset."

And that was the one basic fact at the heart of her personal storm: she shouldn't care whether or not Dev Chandler had squandered his gifts and wasted all the advantages he'd been handed. "What's he doing here, anyway?"

"Visiting our grandmother is a likely guess," Tess said, "considering he's staying in her guest house."

"And?"

"And what?" Tess set the knife aside and arranged lemon slices over a thick, pale fillet in a baking dish.

"And what other little details might have gotten rattled loose and lost in the excitement over the natural disaster this week?" Addie asked.

Tess shot her a sympathetic glance. "It appears he's planning on staying there for a while. Maybe for another month. Or two."

"Great." Addie threw her arms wide, narrowly missing clipping Jack's jaw as she paced the kitchen. "Wonderful. Fantastic. I'll have plenty of opportunities to run into him."

"And plenty of time to quit being so upset." Charlie dried her hands and studied Addie with cool gray eyes. "I thought you were over him."

"I am. But it's a heck of a lot easier being over him when he's living somewhere else."

"You have a thing for Dev Chandler?" Jack asked.

"No," Addie, Charlie and Tess answered in unison.

Tess shoved a platter of chips and salsa to the edge of the table. "So. You're not actually over him. Not really."

"The teensiest of technicalities." Addie plucked one of the chips from the platter and bit into it. "One of several, including the fact that there was never anything to be over in the first place."

Jack pulled a jacket from a rack near the rear patio door and cautiously circled Addie to brush a quick kiss across Charlie's cheek. He headed for the dining room.

"Where are you off to tonight?" asked Tess.

Jack froze. Something suspicious crept along the edges of his smile. "Out."

"Interesting," Tess said. She glanced at Charlie. "Where, precisely, is this 'out' Jack is headed to?"

"Don't be so nosy." Charlie grabbed a bottle of Chardonnay from a cupboard. "It's just a friendly poker game. Quinn invited him."

"Now I'm twice as nosy." Tess narrowed her eyes. "Quinn said exactly the same thing when I asked him where he was going tonight. 'Out.' He told me Jack had invited him."

Addie, Charlie and Tess stared at Jack.

He shrugged into his jacket. "We kind of invited each other. At the same time. When the subject came up."

"How did this subject come up, I wonder?" Tess asked.

"And where is this poker game taking place?" Charlie asked.

"At Chandler House."

"*Dev,*" Addie said.

Jack slid his hands into his pockets. "Yeah, he'll be there, too."

"Convenient." Tess drummed her nails on the table. "Considering the game's at his place."

"This was all his idea, wasn't it?" Addie asked.

"It doesn't matter whose idea it was." Charlie filled a goblet with the wine. "They get a guys' night out. We get a girls' night in. Works for me."

Addie pulled out a chair, dropped into it and reached for more chips. Terrific. Poker games with her friends' fiancés. Poker games would lead to barbecues, and those would lead to who knew what. An ever-expanding network of people who'd multiply the reasons and occasions for her to run into Dev throughout the long summer months.

"Here," Charlie said, handing Addie the glass of Chardonnay. "You look like you could use this."

DEV POPPED THE TOP on a beer Friday night and passed it to his old pal Bud Soames. Hard to picture Bud with thinning hair, a job at a bank, a house undergoing remodeling, a wife in real estate and a kid in elementary school. Nearly made Dev feel like an underachiever.

Each time he'd returned to Carnelian Cove, Dev had found fewer old pals willing to spend a Friday night leaning on the bar at The Shantyman and reminiscing over a few drinks. One by one, the people he'd left behind had moved on to busy lives and expanding responsibilities, building careers and forming families. This time, Dev had decided to skip the lonely bar scene and bring the social hour home.

He glanced at the others gathered around the guest quarters' old kitchen table, its wide oak surface heaped with servings of Julia's layered nachos, crumpled paper napkins, whiskey glasses, beer bottles and poker chips. Jack Maguire and Quinn, owners of their own businesses and both soon to be married. Rusty Wheeler, an expert machinist and builder on Quinn's construction crew. Although Rusty was single, like Dev, he at least had a mortgage. And a dog.

Dev didn't have so much as a goldfish.

"Where are you taking Charlie for the honey-moon?" Rusty asked Jack.

"I wanted to take her to Hawaii, but it turns out she's afraid of flying." Jack tipped back in his chair, his cards close to his chest and a wide grin on his face. It was obvious Jack loved the game, especially bluffing. And even though Dev suspected what he was up to—most of the time, anyway—it was hard not to fall for that drawl and the "aw, shucks" act. "I'm finding out all sorts of fascinating things about my fiancée," Jack said.

"Wedding jitters." Quinn shook his head. "Tess has already thrown a couple of fits, and ours is still a ways off."

"Tess throws a fit at least once a week," Dev pointed out. "She used to say it beat going to the gym."

"Watching her work up a fuss can be pretty entertaining, once you figure out she's just keeping her temper tuned up. Rosie thinks so, anyway." Quinn studied his cards, his expression impossible to read. He played poker the way he seemed to do everything else—with quiet, intense efficiency. Of all the players at the table, he had the least to say and the most chips in his pile. He folded and glanced at Jack. "So, where are you taking Charlie?"

"She wants to check out the Tahoe area. We'll do some hiking, some boating." Jack took the pot and scooped his winnings into his pile. "Maybe go to a couple of shows down in Reno."

"Sounds like fun." Rusty shoved a fresh stick of gum in his mouth and dealt. "I won a couple of hundred at the blackjack tables last time I was there."

"After you'd lost four," Bud reminded him. Bud was

all about keeping track of the winnings and playing it safe.

Dev glanced at his cards. Another lucky hand. He could continue to coast, which suited him fine.

"Where are you staying?" Rusty fanned his cards, frowned and chewed his gum faster—which told everyone at the table he liked what he saw. "Somewhere near the lake?"

"A private estate, right on the north shore. Nice dock, tennis court, maid service." Jack signaled for another card. "The owner's an old friend of mine."

Dev was learning Jack had dozens of "old friends" up and down the state. And he'd managed to make plenty of new friends in Carnelian Cove in the short time he'd been there. The guy had a natural gift for pleasing people. If he ever chose to run for public office, he'd be hard to beat.

"I took Caroline down to Cancún." Bud shook his head. "Man, was that a mistake. She couldn't handle the food or the sun. Spent most of her time in the bathroom, and when she came out she wouldn't let me touch her."

Dev won the pot, as he'd expected.

"Where does Tess want to go?" Rusty asked.

"We haven't discussed it." Quinn shuffled the deck. "We can't go anywhere until Tidewaters is finished. And we'll have to wait until Rosie has a long school holiday."

"Kids." Rusty shook his head as Quinn dealt. "They sure do complicate everything."

"You've been around, Dev." Bud gestured with his bottle. "Where would you go?"

Dev thought of all the places he'd seen that most

people probably considered romantic destinations. Fiji. Paris. The Bahamas. The Greek Isles. Rio, Monte Carlo, Marrakesh, Bali. He imagined any place would seem special, as long as he was there with the right woman. "I'd ask my bride where she wanted to go."

"Well, duh." Bud set his bottle down with a clunk and picked up his cards. "It was Caroline who picked out Mexico."

"Been to Jamaica?" Rusty asked Dev.

"Yeah."

"I've always wanted to go to Jamaica."

"Why?"

"I don't know. Just do, that's all."

They played in silence for a few minutes. Quinn won a small pot, and Bud swept up the cards to shuffle.

"Heard Addie Sutton came by here the other day to see about some broken windows." Bud glanced at Dev as he picked up a chip for the ante. "You still got a thing for her?"

The action around the table stilled. Tweaked in midtoss, Dev's chip went wide and landed on Quinn's plate of half-eaten nachos.

"You and Addie?" Jack tipped the front of his chair back to the floor. "Since when?"

"Since high school." Bud blundered on, dealing the next hand, unaware of the daggers Dev was shooting at him across the table. "Or maybe before."

"I didn't know that." Rusty's chewing slowed to a stop. "You never took her out on a date or anything."

"Didn't have to," Bud said. "They practically lived together."

"Her mother was Geneva's maid," Rusty explained for Jack's benefit.

"Awkward." Jack studied Dev, a curious expression on his face. "Still awkward, I s'pose."

Dev shrugged. He wished he could shrug off the sneaking suspicion that he looked the way he felt: like a teen with a crush. "We're friends. Sort of."

Quinn gave Dev one of his neutral, level stares. "Hard for a single guy to be friends with a woman like that."

"Like Addie?"

"Like a single guy. Who's a 'friend.' *Sort of.*" Quinn lifted his soda can and stared at Dev over the rim. "Addie's had some tough breaks. She doesn't need any more."

"I'm not out to make things difficult for her," Dev said.

"Didn't say you were."

Dev met Quinn's stare and raised him one eyebrow. "Nice to know she's got people here looking out for her."

"Yeah." Quinn nodded, smiling. "One of them is Tess."

"And another is Charlie," Jack pointed out.

While a round of bets were laid, Dev winced at the thought of two of the toughest women he knew coming after him. One more reason to steer clear of Addie.

"Although," Jack added in his most leisurely drawl, "neither of them seemed all that concerned about Addie's feelings on the matter earlier this evening."

Rusty shrugged. "Maybe that's because Addie's still got a crush on Dev."

This time, Dev's chip slid across the table and over the edge, landing on the floor beside Bud's chair. Addie had once had a crush? On him? How could he have missed that? Unless…

Bud sighed as he leaned down to retrieve the chip. "Are we going to play poker or chat all night like a bunch of girls?"

"This isn't girl talk," Rusty pointed out. "It's not like we're gossiping."

"Men don't gossip." Quinn tossed down his cards. "They discuss."

"Damn right." Rusty neatened his stack of chips.

Bud raised the bet, tapping his cards on the edge of the table. "So can we discuss something other than Addie and Dev and whether they're still mooning over each other the way they were in high school?"

"Mooning?" If Jack's grin got any wider, it would split his face in half.

"There was no mooning." Dev quickly looked to Rusty for confirmation.

"No mooning," Rusty agreed with a teasing smile that said otherwise. "Must have been mistaken about Addie, too."

Dev scowled at his cards and folded.

"Calling it quits so soon?" Jack shook his head at Dev as he revealed another bluff and scooped the chips into his pile. "You need to pay more attention. Might want to rethink your strategy, while you're at it."

Dev picked up a few of his chips and let them slide through his fingers. He'd been playing it safe for far too long, relying on his luck to get him through. Now he wondered who'd been bluffing whom all these years.

CHAPTER FOUR

DEV HUNCHED OVER his laptop late Saturday morning, scrolling through his notes and inserting random thoughts in parentheses. Eventually the pages would transform into something resembling an outline for a story; right now, they looked as though they'd been partially composed in code, with ellipses and dashes and chunks of text in boldly colored fonts. It was his method of organizing his thoughts and themes in the misty early stages as the piece lurched and stumbled toward coherence.

He'd intended to write a unique piece of literary fiction—a clever story with bit of homage to film noir, a tale of mystery and murder set in his adopted city of San Francisco. But somehow the setting had shifted north, to a town suspiciously similar to the Cove. And the story had wormed its way inside him to sweep dim, flickering beams over the shadowy places in his past. Cobweb-filled corners he hadn't yet decided he was prepared to examine.

Literary noir was turning out to be a dark and depressing business, indeed.

"Shit," he muttered, as he read the lines he'd just tapped on the keyboard. "Geneva is going to disown me."

The thought of his demanding grandmother had him glancing at his watch. "Shit," he said again as he saved his notes and closed the laptop. He was expected for a coffee-break meeting in her office this morning, and he was running late. Tardiness was near the top of a long list of faults and weaknesses for which Geneva had little patience.

He ran a hand across his chin before stepping into the black-and-white tiled bath. He could cut some time by skipping the morning's shave. Second day in a row, and the stubble had stepped up to whisker stage, so he might catch one of his grandmother's sharp and frosty glares. But that was better than catching another pithy reminder about the importance of promptness.

His thoughts drifted with the shower steam, fragments of story ideas and pieces of memories tumbling together as the scalding water pummeled his body. Writing had always been his scholastic ace in the hole, so he'd followed the path of least resistance and studied journalism in a San Francisco-area college.

After graduation, he'd pleased his family and postponed steady—and suffocatingly routine—employment by pursuing an advanced degree in English. And after that, it had been an easy slide into a part-time position as a lecturer teaching basic writing courses to first-year students at the same university.

The pay wasn't great, but he didn't need much. After his father had been killed during Dev's junior year of college, Dev had handed a few chunks of his inheritance to friends in the electrical engineering program, and those investments in software development had brought him far more than the funds tucked away in the family trust.

Nothing earned, plenty gained—the one consistent pattern to his life. And since it seemed to be working, he'd gone with the flow. Without much effort, he'd created a laid-back lifestyle that suited him down to his scuffed loafers. Part-time work, part-time play, part-time friends. Part-time lovers, when he was willing to expend the effort on the mating ritual. A low-maintenance rental when he was in the city, some low-key travel when he was in the mood for different views and experiences.

But lately he'd grown bored explaining the thesis statement, critiquing freshmen essays, avoiding committee work and dating as casually as possible. And the slightly cynical entries that he read in some of his students' journals made him feel as though he was stuck with them in player mode, trapped in an endless and self-indulgent adolescence. He was too young for a midlife crisis and too old to be making short-term career plans and the same moves on the opposite sex he'd been making since he was an undergrad.

He was itching for a change, eager for a challenge. Taking his talent for writing more seriously seemed as good a place to start as any. He didn't even have to quit his job to do it, since his teaching stint had never been permanent.

He needed to read through his father's papers again. Geneva would resist, at first, but he was certain he'd get his way in the end. She had no reason to deny his request, other than a desire to avoid the memories he'd churn up with his poking and prodding. Memories of his father's final days, of the accident that had claimed his life and the scandal that had briefly flared before fading to whispers.

Rubbing a towel over his head, he escaped the jungle-like humidity of the bath. He pulled on a pair of jeans and a navy T-shirt before shoving his feet into scuffed, shapeless loafers. As he exited the guest quarters designed to resemble an old carriage house, he combed his fingers through his hair. A few crunching steps across the parking area, and he headed along the footpath winding through a shadowy redwood grove toward the mansion.

Lingering tatters of morning fog floated around thick ferns sprouting from the springy carpet of auburn bark and needles. The mist caught the sun's rays, spreading them in silvery fans beneath the tangled canopy of redwood branches, vine maples and wild rhododendron. A jay squawked in protest as he disturbed its flight path, and a mule deer bounded into one of the narrow trails leading up the hill. The brine-scented breeze flowing in from the ocean carried the rumble and rush of the surf.

Later today he'd pester Julia for one of her ham-and-cheddar sandwiches and carry that and a couple of bottles of beer down to the tiny cove wedged between the cliffs. He'd sit with his back against a sun-warmed rock, plow his toes into the cold sand and let his thoughts drift, just like old times.

Old times. He'd laughed and winced over a few of those last night with Rusty and Bud. Drag races on the beach, exploding mailboxes, blackened eyes, broken hearts. Parties that had gone on too long and too loud. He'd probably turned Geneva's hair gray ahead of schedule.

He paused at the edge of the grove to admire the mansion that came into view. His great-grandfather had worked his way from lumberjack to mill owner, buying this land and laying the foundation for the family fortune. His grandfather had made a series of brilliant business investments in Carnelian Cove and built Chandler House to showcase his success.

Dev's father, Jonah, had knocked a few holes in the walls.

Jonah may have had an obsession for work and several lofty ambitions, but he hadn't inherited his parents' business sense. And now Dev had come back to this house to find out what had really happened nine years ago. To read through his father's papers, to try to unravel the lingering mysteries about the night of Jonah's death and the days following, when the extent of his father's carelessness in overseeing the family business interests had been revealed.

Skirting the open service-parking area, Dev detoured to the south side of the house, entering through the conservatory doors. Water dripped from copper-lined planters to pool on the slate beneath, and a tiny green frog leaped for cover beneath a waxy begonia leaf as he passed. The scents of loam and violets rode on the humid air.

Moving quickly through the formal rooms, Dev made his way to the entry hall and paused near the wide marble steps leading from the main entry. The ugly plywood sheets standing in for the missing windows were a shock, two blackened gaps like missing teeth between the jewel-like morning light streaming through the glass on either side.

He grinned over the memory of Addie's efforts to maintain control of the situation two days ago. If she'd known how transparent she'd been, how easy it had been to read every emotion in her lovely features, her cheeks would have burned as pink as the roses in the windows she'd had transported to her shop.

Addie Sutton, businesswoman. He'd always known she had a talent for art. He had to admire the way she'd used it to make a life for herself.

There was a lot to admire there.

A familiar uneasiness swept over him, from the restless shuffle of his feet on the marble floor to the faint pressure in his chest, which he tried to ease with a shift of his shoulders. The talk around the poker table had him recalling an earlier memory. A memory of Addie standing at the grassy end of the high school parking lot as he'd rumbled by in his car, of the way she'd lowered her head and peered at him from beneath her lashes. Just for an instant, like the click of a camera shutter, he'd witnessed in her features the same emotion that had smoldered deep inside him.

And then there'd been a tug, as if he were a fish on a line, as if he'd swallowed the bait so deep an escape would rip out his guts. It would have been so easy to let her reel him in. It would have been so easy to stop, to roll down his window and offer her a ride. They were headed in the same direction, after all.

But Bud had jogged over, hopped in the passenger side and leaned on the horn, trying to catch the attention of another girl across the lot. Addie had jerked and dropped her books on the grass, her cheeks burning and her hands clumsy as she gathered them. And Dev had sped away, ashamed for so many reasons and blaming Addie for most of them.

A high-pitched growl brought him back to the present. One of Geneva's yippy little dogs edged close to sniff at his loafers, the silly blue bow tied to a tuft of fur on its head quivering in outrage. "The scouting expedition," Dev muttered.

He started down the dim hall toward Geneva's office, and the rest of the pack of Yorkies swarmed around his ankles and raised the alarm as he entered the room.

Geneva silenced the dogs with a wave of her hand. "Good morning, Devlin."

He bent to press a kiss against her soft gray hair. "Good morning, Grandmother."

She lifted one elegant eyebrow and the pot by her side. "Coffee?"

"Yes. Please." He reached for the cup she handed him and then settled back against downy chair cushions. Julia's coffee was worth the trip from his rooms at this relatively early hour. "What's up?"

Geneva shuddered delicately. "Nothing is *up*. I have a few things to discuss with you before I leave next week."

Dev froze with the cup raised near his chin. "You're going somewhere?"

"I've decided to accept an old friend's invitation for a cruise in the Caribbean. I'll be flying to San Francisco the morning after my annual Fourth of July picnic to do some shopping and to make a call on your Aunt Jacqueline before I leave for the gulf."

Aunt Jacqueline. Dev had lived in the same city, and yet he hadn't seen Tess's mother for years. "Why didn't you mention this before I decided to come up here for a visit?"

"You needn't bother sounding so wounded, Devlin. You'll embarrass us both." Geneva sipped her coffee.

"I assume you didn't make the trip north just to visit me."

"Why else would I be here?"

"That's one of the things I'd like to discuss this morning."

His grandmother may have been nearing eighty, but she remained as observant and shrewd as ever. He quickly drained his coffee and then leaned forward, his elbows on his knees. "I want another look at Dad's papers."

Geneva set her cup aside and folded her hands in her lap. "I can't possibly imagine what purpose that would serve after all these years."

"I'm working on a story angle. I think they might help."

"With a plot element containing striking similarities to the family business? Or some sordid account bearing an uncanny resemblance to the circumstances surrounding your father's death?"

"I would never do that." He settled back against his seat. "I resent the implication that you'd think—even for a second—that I might consider it."

"I'm relieved to hear that. And there was no implication," she said with steel in her voice. "My questions are always clear and direct, as you well know."

He opened his mouth to disagree and to ask a few questions of his own, questions that roiled and bubbled up inside him, but he paused until the hottest spike of temper had subsided. Old patterns, old anger.

Calmer, he chose just one question and cleared his throat to smooth the words. "What do I have to do to prove myself?"

"What is it you're trying to prove, exactly?"

His grandmother waited a beat for his answer, but when she saw there was none coming, she freshened the coffee in her cup and offered him the same. He refused.

"I'd like to know what it is you feel you need to prove to me," she continued, "because I have a favor to ask. And I don't want you to think that granting this favor will somehow count toward proving your worth."

He crossed an ankle over his knee. "You need something from me."

"As it so happens, yes, I do."

"Is this a first?"

"Have you been keeping score?"

The glance she gave him over the rim of her cup sparkled with amusement. Interfering old woman. No one else in his life could fill him with so much frustration, resentment and admiration, all at once. And make his chest constrict so tightly with love. "One of us has to keep score," he said. "For old times' sake."

"Then it should be you, I suppose." She lowered her cup to her lap and turned her face toward the window, her gaze trailing over the bunches of opalescent wisteria dangling through the arbor outside. "I don't have that kind of time to spare."

Her admission troubled him. He'd rarely heard her refer to her age. It was difficult to imagine his life without Geneva Chandler in it. She was like the rocky cliffs beyond the edge of her neatly trimmed lawn, standing tall and rough and defiant, year after year, against the pounding ocean waves.

"You don't have to prove yourself, you know," she said. "I'm quite satisfied with the man you've become. I hope you are, too."

He shifted in his seat and lowered his foot to the floor, more disturbed by her praise than by her disappointment in him. He'd had more practice dealing with the latter. Much more. "I guess I'm doing okay. So far."

She spared him an enigmatic smile and lifted her cup to her lips for another sip. "The favor I'm about to ask stems in part from what I wanted to discuss with you today. I've decided to leave Chandler House to you."

His stomach seemed to rise and lodge in his throat. "I don't want it."

"Then you can do with it as you see fit after I'm gone. It will be your decision."

"Damn." He shoved out of his chair and stalked to the window, staring at that jade-green sweep of lawn, at the ribbony drive leading to the iron gates, and he felt it all weigh on him until he could barely draw breath for his next words. "Is there something you're not telling me?"

"I'm in excellent health, if that's what you're wondering."

"Then why did you choose to discuss this with me now? And why are you giving me Chandler House?" He turned to face her, his fingers gripping the sill. "Why not leave it to Tess? She loves this place."

"Yes, she does. But I'll see to it that she has the means to build a house of her own design. A new house, a unique one. A home that reflects her talents as an architect. She'll prefer that, I'm sure."

"Have you asked her? No, of course not," he said. "She'd have told me."

"The only person I've discussed this with is Ben."

Ben Chandler, Geneva's favorite cousin. Ben would

soon marry her friend, Maudie Keene. Charlie Keene's mother, his new friend Jack's soon-to-be in-law. Incestuous place, Carnelian Cove.

Geneva calmly sipped her coffee. "I notice you haven't asked why the estate won't be inherited by anyone else."

Dev snorted. His grandmother had never disguised her displeasure in her children or their choices. "I don't blame you for skipping a generation," he said.

"No." Geneva's faint sigh hinted of weariness. "There's slightly less…satisfaction there. Besides, I doubt Tess's mother would care to abandon the city's social whirl for the quiet of the Cove. She'd sell this place in a flash."

"And break Tess's heart." He shoved his hands into his pockets. "I could sell it to her."

"To Tess? She wouldn't take it, not like that." Geneva set her cup aside. "Quinn wouldn't let her."

"What makes you think I won't sell it to someone else? Someone outside the family?"

Geneva's mouth curled, catlike, at the edges. "Would you sell it, Devlin?"

He couldn't say it; he couldn't disappoint her. Not again.

Overwhelmed by the challenges of this place—and dreading this favor his grandmother wanted to ask of him—he turned and stared again at the seemingly endless horizon stretching over the countless ocean swells.

"Damn," he whispered.

CHAPTER FIVE

ADDIE FOUND IT INCREASINGLY difficult to stay focused on her task Saturday afternoon. She hunched at her desk, staring at a depressing spreadsheet and gloomy financial projections on her monitor. Manipulating the figures led her to the same conclusions, even with the outrageously high fee she'd charged Geneva as a down payment for her repair work, her business was still listing in a sea of red ink.

She saved and closed her files and refocused on a much more pleasant scene beyond her shop windows. Bathed in soft sunshine and balmy weather, tourists strolled along Cove Street, stopping for a treat at Giulietta's Gelateria or pausing to admire the merchants' displays. It looked as though Cal Penfold's wine shop was enjoying a brisk business today, and Becca Spaulding seemed to be selling quite a lot of her handmade jewelry.

Addie silently willed the browsers to do more than briefly admire her art before moving on. She'd increase her chances of a sale by at least one hundred percent if only someone would open her door and enter.

One young couple stopped and studied a circular piece in a fruitwood frame—a fanciful rainbow trout foiled in copper with a verdigris finish. The man seemed intrigued, pointing out the brilliant colors and the contrasting textures of the seedy-glass fish and the rough-rolled blues Addie had chosen to represent rippling, shimmering water. The woman shook her head, and the couple moved on.

With a silent sigh, Addie stood and stretched some of her tension away. Rather than stare at columns of numbers or dig into repair work or watch potential customers pass her by, she decided to take a break and enjoy the view on the opposite end of her work space.

Mick O'Shaughnessy bent at the waist to measure and mark a length of shelving. His biceps flexed beneath tan skin as the blade buzzed through the wood, and his blond-tipped locks swung over his forehead. He straightened with the short board in hand, winked at her and sidled through the gap in her counter to nail the new piece in place on the sidewall storage bins.

A woman had to appreciate having her very own handyman, especially when he looked and moved like a big, tawny lion, all golden tones and rippling power. She wasn't fooled by his slow and easy manner—she'd seen him in explosive action on the ball field, twisting to make a dramatic catch, bulleting the ball to the infield or smashing a home run into the stands. And she was no longer taken in by his slouchy Texas twang— she'd heard too many examples of his biting wit and keen intellect.

She'd met Mick nearly four weeks earlier, when Jack and Quinn had arranged an outing to the local minor league park. Tess had played matchmaker, and Addie had gone along with her plans. Since then, she and the ballplayer had shared a handful of casual dates and several sweet, lingering kisses. There might have been more between them, but his team had been on the road a great deal, and they both worked long hours.

Which was a thin and shabby excuse.

Mick offered everything a woman should want: kindness, generosity, a sense of humor, a solid work ethic. So why didn't Addie want him as much as she should?

She'd told herself, at first, that she didn't want to become seriously involved with a man who might be leaving Carnelian Cove at the end of the ball season. Now that her two best friends were getting married and settling down, she'd renewed those same goals for herself—with an emphasis on that settling down part. And settling down meant staying here, in the Cove.

But the fact was that she and Mick didn't generate the right kind of heat, that white-hot passion that fused a couple together and promised to keep their bond toasty for the long haul. Still, she liked him well enough to hope he might make the Cove his home. And she cared for him enough to dream their relationship might deepen, that their friendship could somehow catch on fire and move to the next step.

It could happen. Relationships took a lot of work, at times, and it was only reasonable that some of them might need more of that work in the early stages. She was willing to try. Was Mick?

"A penny for your thoughts," he said.

"Huh?" Addie blinked, her cheeks warming as she realized she'd been staring at him. "Oh. Well." She gestured awkwardly at her desk. "I'm not sure I have any pennies to spare."

The bell over her door signaled a customer, and she turned to greet a woman and her young daughter. Mick quietly slipped behind her counter to take a break at her work bench. He sipped from his can of soda while she answered their questions about mosaic supplies and sold them a kit for assembling a pretty mirror frame.

"Given any more thought to those stained-glass lessons you mentioned?" Mick asked after her customers had left. He'd returned to his project, hooking his tape over the edge of a board to measure for another length of shelving. "I know a couple of people who might be interested in signing up."

Addie sank into her desk chair and smoothed a hand over her paperwork. "It's a frustrating situation. I know I'd sell more supplies. And I'd earn some extra money from tuition, of course. But first I'd have to spend some money to get things set up for the class. Money I don't have to spare right now."

"Money for what?" Mick pressed his nail gun against the base of the storage-bins shelf and pulled the trigger. *Whomp.* "Stocking up on those supplies you're going to end up selling anyway?"

"Money for an expanded work area for the students to use. More table surface, more outlets for the irons. Better lighting."

She wandered around her current worktables, visualizing the setup. She'd have to move some boxed inventory into her cramped living quarters temporarily, but she'd gladly sacrifice space for income. "I'd need to replace the bit on one of my old grinders or buy a new machine for the students to use. And I'd need to enlarge the grinder bench to hold it."

"Good thing you know a carpenter."

"Mick." Addie sucked in a deep breath and turned

to face him. "I can't keep relying on you to help me out like this."

"I don't see why not."

"If I can't afford to buy materials, I can't afford the labor."

"How about a trade?" He bent to measure another length of wood. "My mama's birthday is coming up real soon, and I've left my shopping until the last minute, like I always do. You'd be doing me a big favor if you let me take my pick of one of those pretty glass pictures hanging in your window. I'm sure she'd love it."

"None of those pieces is worth as much as what I'd owe you."

He shot her a sly glance as he set the saw for the cut. "How about throwing in the wrapping? And the shipping?"

She waited until the buzzing whine of the saw had stopped. "And a card?" she asked.

"Good idea. That'll save me some shopping time, too."

"You'll have to find the time to sign it."

"Lady, you drive a hard bargain." His grin spread wide. "But you got yourself a deal. Tossing in the card was the clincher."

She sighed, still unconvinced the deal was a fair one. "Which piece did you have in mind?"

He dropped the saw, stepped over the boards and strode to the front of her shop. "This one, right up there." He pointed without a moment's hesitation to a tangle of opalescent irises rising over a rippling blue pond, and Addie quickly figured out he'd been planning on a trade—or a purchase—all along.

"Mama has a bunch of these spiky flowers in her garden," he told her, "so I know she'd like it. If she got something this nice from me, she'd be as happy as a gopher in soft dirt."

"All right then." Addie joined him beneath the displays suspended against her large shop window. "I agree—it's a deal. That bit about the gopher was the clincher. When do you want me to send it?"

His smile turned sheepish. "How about today?"

"When's her birthday?"

"Tuesday."

Addie masked her dismay at the thought of the expense of custom packaging and express shipping for such a fragile item. Still, whatever her costs might be, Mick was the one coming out on the short end of this deal. And he'd be working overtime for her, squeezing this favor in between his part-time work for Quinn Construction and his commitments to his team. "No problem," she said.

"That's my girl." Mick laid one of his big, capable hands on her shoulder and bent to press a quick, affectionate kiss to her cheek as her door clicked open and set the bell above it jingling.

She turned to find Dev in the entry, his hands in his pockets and a strange, unreadable expression on his face. Heat rushed into her cheeks and she froze in place, trapped between embarrassment and annoyance. "Dev."

"Hi."

He flicked a glance over her head at Mick, who had yet to remove his hand from her shoulder…and who had probably felt her body go rigid when she recognized the man who'd entered her shop. Mick's fingers tightened reassuringly.

Possessively.

His hand slid away, in a light stroke down her back, and she cleared her throat. "Dev Chandler, Mick O'Shaughnessy. One of Quinn's crew members. He's, uh, fixing some shelves for me. Dev's an old—" What was he, exactly? She waved a vague, introductory wave in his direction. "He's Tess's cousin."

Dev's mouth twisted in an ironic smile. She shut her mouth before her rambling got out of control.

Mick released her and leaned forward, offering his hand, as casual as could be. Dev took it with a nod.

"What are you doing here?" she asked Dev.

Stupid, stupid, stupid. This is a shop, she reminded herself. And what would Mick think of her squeaky voice and her gawky manners?

"I came to check on the windows," Dev said. "As a favor. For Geneva."

"Oh. Of course."

She flinched when Mick yanked his tape measure from his toolbelt. He stalked back toward his small pile of lumber and sawdust. Dev's gaze tracked his every move.

Addie aimed a thumb over her shoulder. "They're over here."

She stepped behind the counter, into her work space, and waited for Dev to join her there. He followed slowly, scanning the items on her shelves and displays. He'd never been in her shop. Not once, in all these years.

And why would he? It wasn't as though they were old friends, as she'd nearly told Mick. Two people had to be friendly to make that claim.

Tucked into a rear corner, beneath a tall set of

shelves filled with boxes of inventory, stood a neat row of thick foam boards, plywood sheets and crates, all stacked on end. She dragged out one of the large, narrow boxes Quinn had built to protect the windows while they were transported and stored, and pointed to the identifying information scrawled in fat, black lettering. "I won't be able to do much until I get a space cleared," she said as she shoved the container back into place. "They're bigger pieces than I normally work on."

Dev frowned and shoved his hands into his pockets as Mick's saw screamed through another cut, waiting to speak. "What are you going to do to them, exactly?"

"Exactly?" She paused, considering how much detail she wanted to go into with Mick keeping one eye on her and Dev keeping one eye on Mick. "A lot of that depends on what I find when I start to take them apart."

"Apart?"

Whomp, whomp, whomp. Mick's nail gun fastened one more narrow edging strip to the front of the remodeled storage bins.

She nodded. "I can't simply cut a new piece of glass to replace the broken one and slip it back into place. I've got to start at one side and work my way in, piece by piece, dismantling the caming until I reach the area that needs the repair."

"Caming." Dev paused to watch Mick stretch his tape measure across a board. "Is that the lead?"

"Yes."

"Sounds like taking a corner of a puzzle apart to try to reach a piece near the middle."

"Exactly."

"Do you work on repairs at night?"

"No." She shook her head and waited through another of Mick's noisy cuts. "I have plenty of time during regular shop hours to do repair work. Not that I don't have lots of other business to keep me busy," she added quickly. The last thing she wanted Dev to know was how precarious things were at times.

Most of the time.

"I'll have to get started on the windows for Tess's project soon," she said. "Those will keep me tied up for months. And I'll need still more space for those, too."

"How long does it take you to make a window—a window of the size Tess has in mind?" he asked.

She stared at Dev, trying to decipher that strange new element in his expression—that odd, banked heat. If she didn't know him better, she'd think he was interested in her. Or in what she was saying. But he couldn't possibly be.

So why was he sticking around for so long and asking so many questions? "Why do you want to know? Did Geneva send you to spy on me?"

"No." His eyes creased at the corners, reminding her how she used to hate feeling as though she was the butt of his private jokes. "I'm just curious," he said.

A customer walked into her shop, and she excused herself to greet him. Dev stayed where she'd left him, watching her pull a couple of lengths of caming from a shelf and stretch a few pieces before ringing up the sale.

"Now I'm really curious," Dev said after she'd returned to the rear of her shop. "What did you do with those strips of metal?"

"I stretched them."

"Why?"

"It has to do with the molecules in the lead." She crossed her arms and leaned against her worktable. "If you're really interested, I could explain it all in detail. Some other time, maybe."

She tightened her fingers on her arms, holding herself steady beneath the scrutiny of that stomach-knotting, crinkly-cornered stare.

"Okay," he said at last. "Some other time, then."

She walked him to the door. "Please tell Geneva I'll get to work on her windows as soon as the replacement glass arrives. I want to make sure I've got everything I need before I start."

Dev pulled the door open and then paused, shifting slightly, his face a few inches from hers. "Anything else you'd like to say?" he asked in a low, intimate tone.

She bit her lower lip and shook her head.

He cast one last, dark glance in Mick's direction before pulling the door closed behind him.

Addie was tempted to sag against the jamb. Instead, she placed a palm on the door and curled her fingers against the cool glass as she watched Dev moving quickly down the street with his long, confident stride. She was relieved to see him go. And wishing she'd taken the chance to say…something.

"You don't like that guy much, do you?" Mick asked.

"I'm sorry it was so obvious. That must have been uncomfortable for you." She pushed her hair back from her face with a sigh. "Dev Chandler seems to bring out the worst in me. He always has."

"How long have you known each other?"

"Since we were kids." She crossed the shop to

admire the new bins Mick had installed. "His dad brought him to live at Chandler House when I was eight. He's been tormenting me ever since. Like a nasty big brother."

Mick narrowed his eyes. "He doesn't think of you as a sister."

"Well, I'm not his sister, thank goodness. This is wonderful, Mick," she said, running her hand along the smooth edge of a new bin divider. A slight downward tilt to the base would prevent the glass squares from shifting forward and falling during another quake. "Perfect. Thank you."

"Easy as pie." He unstrapped his utility belt and dropped it in his toolbox. "A couple coats of paint, and you're all set."

"That chore can wait until tomorrow." She checked her watch before flipping the sign in her shop door to Closed. "Another day closer to retirement."

Mick stooped to toss wood scraps into the box Addie handed to him. "What do you think you'll do when that day comes?"

"Probably the same things I do now," she said as she swept sawdust into a pan. "Only I'll be retired, so they'll be just for fun."

"That's a nice way of looking at it. You're a ray of sunshine, aren't you?" He stepped closer, and ran a fingertip down the side of her face. "I sure do like that about you, Addie."

She forced herself to stand very still, to appreciate his touch and absorb the sweetness of his gesture. "What will you do when you retire?" she asked.

"Settle some place where the summers are long and warm and I can get season tickets to the local ballpark.

Going to sit in the stands on game nights and out on my front porch on the nights in between."

"Sounds wonderful."

He lowered his gaze to his boots and scrubbed one toe over a crack in her concrete floor. "Coming to the game tonight?"

She was careful to keep her smile in place as she moved away to put the broom back in its place. "Going to leave a ticket for me at the gate?"

"Going to have a drink with me after the game if I do?"

"Going to hit a home run for me if I say yes?"

"Now darlin'," he said with a put-upon sigh, "you know I can't deliver one of those babies every game."

"I'm not asking about every game." She closed her cash box and locked it away in a file drawer. "Just the ones I come to watch."

"Then it's a good thing you don't travel with the team."

He coiled the extension cord he'd brought and dumped it into the box with his tools. "Are you sure you don't want me to add a little piece of trim to the front edges of those shelves and dividers? It wouldn't—"

"I can't afford anything fancy. And no," she said, holding up a hand to halt the argument she knew was coming, "you're not going to toss it in for free. You've already spent way more time on this than I'd figured. I can't take advantage of your generosity like that."

"You don't seem to mind taking my free game passes," he said with a wink. "Of course, I don't mind handing them out to such a pretty fan."

"I am a fan." She walked willingly into the arms he'd

spread wide and wrapped her arms around his waist. "And it's not just 'cause you're a terrific ballplayer."

"I'm a mighty terrific carpenter, too."

"Yes, you are." She rested the side of her face against his warm T-shirt, listening to the strong, steady beat of his heart. "And a fine human being."

Beneath her cheek, his chest raised and lowered on a long sigh. And then he lifted a hand and softly stroked her hair. "I'm not usually one to find fault with such a nicely phrased compliment, but when a woman starts lumping me in with humanity in general, I have to wonder if I've slipped a couple of notches in her list of priorities."

Addie stilled. "I don't know what to say."

"You know, my daddy has a saying for just about every situation you could name. Right about now he'd probably say, 'You can put your boots in the oven, but that don't make 'em biscuits.'"

She laughed and drew away, gazing up at Mick's smiling face. "I love your Texas sayings."

"But not the man saying them. It's all right, Addie girl." He gently grabbed her arms when she tried to pull out of his. "I figured this talk's been coming on for quite some time now. I knew it for sure when I saw you with Dev Chandler."

Mick released her, and she backed away, shaking her head in denial. "You said yourself I don't like him much."

"No, I asked you how you feel about him."

"And I told you he brings out the worst in me."

"Ever ask yourself why that is?"

"It's…there's…" She huffed out an impatient breath. "I don't want to think about it. Not tonight, anyway."

She stepped in closer to Mick and placed her palms against his chest. "I wish things had worked out differently. Why can't things be simpler?"

"Not even my daddy would have a saying to answer that question." Mick took her hands in his. "Going to join me for a drink after the game?"

"You buying?"

"Tell you what. If I don't hit a homer, the drinks are on me. But if I do, lady, you owe me a beer."

She smiled and nodded. "It's a deal."

He squeezed her hands and let her go.

Addie waited as he finished loading his toolbox, followed him to her door and then tipped up on her toes to brush a goodbye kiss across his cheek. "See you later, Mick."

He stepped outside and walked to his truck, a big, handsome man with broad shoulders, an easy gait and a way of making a woman feel cherished. She stood at her window, watching him drive away, and waited for her heart to break, just a little.

But nothing happened. One dark blast from the past had proved she'd been fooling herself. She couldn't wish deeper emotions into existence.

Or wish them into disappearing.

CHAPTER SIX

When the bell over her door jangled early Sunday afternoon, Addie glanced up from a repair on an oval door window, hoping to see a customer. Instead, Charlie charged inside, a wide grin on her face. "I found a dress!"

"Let me see." Addie grabbed the tattered magazine page Charlie pulled from her jeans pocket and straightened it over a clean space beside the window. "Oh, it's you. It's absolutely you. I *love* it."

"I do, too." Charlie dropped onto one of Addie's work stools. "I thought I'd never find anything that wasn't poofy or frilly or lacy or shiny, or too long or too tight or too—"

"I know." Addie smiled. "I've been there." She studied the picture more closely, admiring the simple A-line chiffon with darling capped sleeves and subtle detailing on a modest bodice. "But this is beautiful. Perfect. Definitely worth all the looking."

"If you say so." Charlie took back the page, staring at the model and worrying her lower lip. "At least it doesn't cost as much as most of those gowns. What a waste of—"

"You only get to be a bride once in your life. And Maudie will only get to be the mother of the bride once in hers. She said she wanted to spoil you—let her do it." Addie stepped behind Charlie to peer over her shoulder at the gown. "Has she seen this yet?"

"She's the one who found it."

"Go, Maudie."

"Yeah. She's been freaked out I'd never find anything I liked in time for the wedding." Charlie ran a finger over a crease. "I wonder what Tess will think."

"The same thing I do." Addie wrapped her arms around her friend's shoulders and gave her a happy, excited hug. "She'll think it's gorgeous. And you'll be gorgeous in it."

Charlie snorted. "All I care about is that I'll be wearing a fancy white dress, and now everyone can breathe a sigh of relief."

"You've still got to decide on a veil, if you're wearing one. And how you'll fix your hair. And shoes—you'll need to find some special shoes."

"Come on, let me off the hook for the rest of the day, will you? You can start nagging me about all that other stuff tomorrow." Charlie folded the page, leaned to the side and stuffed it into her pocket. "I heard the Wildcats won their game last night."

"It wasn't even close." Addie moved back to her work stool and picked up her soldering iron. "Mick hit another home run."

Charlie leaned her elbows on the table and waggled her eyebrows. "Did he hit one after the game, too?"

"Not exactly." Addie brushed flux over the joint and then touched the iron to the solder, melting the metal before scrubbing it away. She dreaded disappointing Charlie on the day she'd decided on her wedding dress. "I don't think we'll be seeing each other again. Not socially, anyway."

"Aw, Addie." Charlie blew out a long, unhappy sigh. "What happened? Did you two have a fight?"

"No." Addie ran the iron over a curve, melting another joint. "There wasn't anything much to fight about—that was part of the problem." She wiped the tip of the iron on the little chunk of wet sponge on the holder, watching a wisp of steam rise and tiny spatters of molten solder skitter across the blackened surface. "No heat."

"But you two were such a good couple."

"We were, weren't we?" Addie picked up her brush and scrubbed bits of metal from the caming, remembering the first time she'd seen Mick—loping out to left field, wearing the sun on his hair and a grin on his face. Making an amazing catch, making her heart skip with possibilities. "He's such a sweetheart. I wish I could have talked myself into loving him. But the harder I tried, the more I knew I wasn't being fair to either of us."

"You're feeling this way because Dev's back in town, aren't you?" Charlie jumped from her stool to pace around the worktable. "This is all his doing, isn't it?"

"No," Addie said after a second's hesitation. "Not exactly."

"What do you mean, *exactly?*"

"He came in yesterday, while Mick was here fixing my storage bins."

"Sounds like something he'd pull."

"*Charlie.*" Addie set down her brush with a sigh. "He didn't know Mick would be here. He didn't even know about Mick."

Embarrassment and regret washed through Addie as she remembered how quickly Dev had figured things out. How flustered and confused and clumsy she'd felt as he stood there, staring at her in that curious way. How her reactions to Dev's presence must have hurt Mick, if only a little.

She'd relived those moments, over and over, through the night and again this morning. And wondered what she was going to do—how she was going to deal with Dev if he suspected she was attracted to him.

"That's no excuse." Charlie squinted with suspicion. "What was Dev doing here in the first place?"

"He came to check on the window repair."

"Is that what he told you?"

"Yes."

Charlie threw her arms wide. "And you believed him?"

"Why shouldn't I?"

"Because he won't leave you alone, and he always hurts you. He's always been nothing but trouble for you."

Addie leaned forward, fisting a hand over her heart. "I made that trouble for myself." And oh, how the truth hurt. It punched her in the stomach and stung her eyes. But it was time she faced it and dealt with it. She'd cocooned herself in layer upon layer of daydreams about an impossible future with a man who'd never—not once, in all these years—shown any real interest in her.

"You're defending him," Charlie pointed out, "just like you always do. The same way you stick up for everybody."

Addie struggled to get her response past the hot knot in her throat. "You make me sound like a doormat."

"No, that's not what I meant." Charlie strode toward the nearest counter. "But you've always been too nice for your own good. Too generous, too patient. Always looking for the best in everyone. Good ol' Addie, every—"

Charlie cut her rant short when she turned and caught Addie dashing away a tear. "Oh, Addie, I didn't mean it," she said, rushing around the table to wrap her in a clumsy hug. "You're rotten. Rotten to the core. Most of the time, I hate your guts."

Addie sputtered through a choking laugh. "You're just saying that to be nice."

"Nice? Me?" Charlie gave Addie's shoulders a squeeze. "Now I know you're upset."

Addie sniffed hugely and shook her head. "I'm not as upset as I should be. About Mick, I mean. And that tells me I did the right thing."

"If you say so."

Charlie dragged a stool closer to Addie and took a seat. "I wish there was something I could do."

"I appreciate that."

"Yeah, well, you'd appreciate it a lot more if I actually did something other than make you cry."

"You didn't make me cry. I did that to myself. And I feel much better now." Addie sucked in a deep, cleansing breath and then rubbed a hand over Charlie's shoulder. "And you're here, keeping me company on your day off and listening to all my troubles. You're a good friend. I'm lucky to have you."

"There you go again." Charlie shook her head. "Comforting someone who doesn't need it as much as you do."

"We could talk about what kind of a veil would match that dress. And hairstyles." Addie scrubbed her cheeks with the heels of her hands. "That would cheer me up."

"Good ol' Addie." Charlie scowled. "Always looking for a silver lining."

THOUGH MONDAY MORNINGS didn't necessarily start a new workweek for Dev—particularly during term breaks—he'd decided long ago to treat them that way.

Sort of. Sometimes.

So it was with a number of worthwhile intentions that he rolled out of bed an hour after his alarm went off. Lingering over his morning coffee, he enjoyed the first several chapters of a novel he'd picked up in the bookstore near the marina. After a long, steamy shower, he stretched his legs with a hike down to the beach before raiding Julia's pantry for brunch supplies. By the time noon arrived, he was primed to be productive: to make a meaningful start on that story he planned to finish by summer's end.

But first he'd make a trip to town. Knowing there were errands to be done could trash a writer's concentration and interfere with story development.

Especially errands like this one. When a guy couldn't get a woman out of his mind, that was a huge distraction. The worst kind of interference with the creative process, Dev told himself as he turned a corner and started down Cove Street toward A Slice of Light.

Just to see if Addie's shop was open today.

And why wouldn't it be open on a Monday during the tourist season?

Yep, she was there, he saw as he drove past her shop door. Lights on, sign in door window. Perfect chance to stop in and say hello.

Again.

What had he been thinking, coming here again so soon? It had only been a couple of days since his last surprise visit—what kind of progress could she possibly have made on Geneva's windows in such a short amount of time? Just because his grandmother had handed him the perfect excuse to drop by, he couldn't keep using checks on the repairs as the reasons for his visits. Addie would think he was making a pest of himself, and she'd be right.

But he still needed to see her. To get her out of his head.

He took a short trip around the block and aimed again for her shop. Slowing near an open spot at the curb, he flipped on his signal and angled close to the car ahead to begin the proper parallel parking procedure. And then he shifted back to Drive and pulled away, wondering if Addie had witnessed that knuckleheaded maneuver through one of her big shop windows.

What in the hell would he have said to her after he'd walked in? After hello—then what? Nice day, isn't it? How's business so far today?

Interested in striking up our old friendship while I'm in town this summer?

Except they'd never been friends, not really. Not when he'd found her in Julia's kitchen and they'd sat in silence, feasting on milk and cookies. Not in those moments they'd passed each other in the crowded school hallways and murmured quiet acknowledgements. Not even when he'd fixed her broken locker, or she'd painted a sign for his club's homecoming booth.

Had he imagined some connection that hadn't been there at all?

You need to pay more attention.

No, he hadn't imagined the flare of heat in her eyes that day she'd dropped her books near the school parking lot. And he hadn't imagined the evidence of that same heat in her cheeks when he'd stopped by last week. He'd felt that same awareness. Felt that same yearning to…be with her.

Might want to rethink your strategy, while you're at it. Yeah, Jack had been right about that, too. He turned a corner and found himself making another pass down Cove Street. Even his subconscious was driving him to her door. Might as well go in.

Or not.

He stepped on the gas and accelerated past her shop. God. Had she seen him again? She'd think he was stalking her.

Which might not be far from the truth.

With a curse, he gripped on the wheel and made a sharp turn, bumping one wheel over the curb as he entered the tiny public lot a block away. He took the last available space, switched off the ignition and slumped in his seat. Staring out the windshield, he waited for the mortification to subside and for some rational thought process to take its place.

Why Addie Sutton? Why had seeing her again after all these years unleashed the ghosts of high school past? She'd made it clear she didn't want to see him, wasn't comfortable around him. Hell, there was another guy in the picture, even though she'd denied it. So why did he keep setting himself up for rejection?

Maybe because he had such a talent for it. His mother had left him behind, his father had virtually ignored him. He suspected most of his friends here in the Cove had tolerated him only because of his last name and the money he always had in his wallet.

Break out the violins. Dev Chandler, healthy and wealthy—if none too wise—was indulging in a hell of a pity fest.

Calling it quits so soon?

Not quits. Not exactly. Just playing it safe. This was too important to bluff his way through.

Tess would slap some sense back in him, he decided as he climbed from his car. He rammed his hands into his pockets and stalked around the corner, heading for her Main Street office. Tess had always been good at tossing advice like darts. She'd poked at him plenty of times during those vacation weeks she'd come to stay at Chandler house.

He strode through the door of her architectural design business and then stopped short. Charlie Keene was sitting behind Tess's desk, her muddy work boots propped on the rungs of a visitor's chair. She'd been an irritating part of his life ever since he'd moved into Chandler House—the daughter of Geneva's friend, the friend of the housekeeper's daughter. The snotty little brother he'd never had. And though he'd never done anything to hurt her—that he could recall—it seemed the redheaded runt had always had it in for him.

He'd never understood what sweet, gentle Addie had in common with her two prickly best friends.

"Well," Charlie said with a sneer, "look who came to pay a call."

"Can it, Keene."

"No problem. I'm not in the mood to make small talk with small people."

"And I'm not in the mood to listen to you two claw

at each other," Tess said as she stepped from a storage area, struggling to maneuver a large model on its oversize board past a brick wall. "Not this afternoon, anyway."

She set the model on the desk, in front of Charlie. "Tell me what you think."

"I think it looks expensive."

Dev stepped closer, studying the form. A series of steep shed roofs rose and fell in an intriguing saw-tooth pattern, providing plenty of spaces for high windows that would flood the interior area with light. Still more windows were set two-by-two in a complementary pattern of zigzagging corners. Strikingly clean lines, plenty of interesting angles and a clever way to maximize a view. "What is it?" he asked.

"It's a new office building for Keene Concrete." Tess turned the model to show a side view. "It's time that business moved out of its rusting office trailer and started looking like it's going to stick around awhile."

Charlie frowned and poked at one of the roof peaks. "Did Jack put you up to this?"

"No." Tess flicked away a stray bit of paper stuck to one corner of the board. "Maudie mentioned she wouldn't mind a bigger office, and when—"

"And when my mom just happened to mention she wanted more space, you thought you'd take the opportunity to drum up some business for yourself."

"No harm in planning ahead." Tess shrugged. "And no foul if you don't like this first plan—although I do hope you like the general look, since I think it's a good one. If you like it enough, we can discuss an interior layout. And the materials," she added, warming to her subject. "I'd love to work with as much rock as possible, although I think we should use local redwood, too."

"Our customers are going to think we're charging them too much." Charlie folded her arms on Tess's desk and rested her chin on her hands, examining the front more closely. "But it sure is nice."

"Of course it's nice," Tess said. "It's perfect. And extremely attractive, considering the site is essentially light industrial." She pointed to the row of angled corner windows. "This is the section that will overlook the river. You'll notice every office space has a two-directional view. And here," she added, turning the model again, "are the main entry and the windows facing the plant."

"Has Jack seen this yet?" Charlie asked.

"No."

"Good. Do me a favor and don't show him until after the wedding." Charlie stood and made her way to the office door, sparing Dev a slit-eyed look as she passed by. "I don't want him nagging me about this on our honeymoon."

"She loves it." Tess's face lit up with a brilliant smile after Charlie had slammed the door behind her. "I knew she would."

"How can you tell?"

"She didn't have any complaints, did she?" Tess cleared a spot on one of her display cubes and carried the model to its new home. "And she said it was nice."

Dev stepped beside her, leaning down to study her handiwork. "This isn't nice. This is amazing. It's all amazing." He glanced at her over his shoulder. "Every once in a while I drive by that little shopping center you did—the one in Palo Alto. It still looks as beautiful as the day it was finished."

"Thanks." Tess stroked a hand down his arm. "A girl can never have enough admirers in her life."

"You've picked up a couple since I saw you last."

"Speaking of picking up," she said, checking her watch, "I've got to collect Rosie from day camp in about twenty minutes."

Dev shook his head. "Never pictured you as the instant family type."

"Never pictured it myself." Tess brushed her short bangs from her eyes. "Life—and love—doesn't always turn out the way we planned it."

"I can't picture Charlie and Jack Maguire together, either."

"They may seem like opposites on the surface, but they've actually got a lot in common, besides the business experience. And if you saw them together, you'd see how much they love each other. It's beautiful." Tess stepped back to admire her creation. "As beautiful as the new Keene Concrete office is going to be."

Dev stared at the model on a neighboring display cube. "Guess I'll get a chance to see them together at Geneva's Fourth of July party."

"Are you staying for that?"

"I'm staying for the summer." He slipped his hands into his pockets and wandered across Tess's office to look at the plans she'd framed and hung on one of the brick walls. "You knew that. I remember telling you, the first night I arrived."

"Yes, but—" Tess laced her fingers together at her waist. "You never stay as long as you say you're going to."

No, he'd never been able to tolerate Geneva's stern

looks or her dictatorial manner for more than a few days at a time. He'd suffered enough of her standards and rules during the years she'd been his surrogate mother; now that he was an adult with his own preferences and habits, he found it easier to slip away than to challenge her in her own home. "I don't have your patience," he told Tess.

"With Mémère, you mean." Tess sank into her desk chair and leaned back, crossing her long legs. "I wonder sometimes if I'm becoming too much like her."

"There's a lot to admire there."

"And a lot to fear."

He settled into the visitor's chair, stretching his legs over Tess's glossy wood floor and crossing his ankles. "You'll have a happier life than grandmother did," he said, thinking of the tragedies that had plagued the Chandler clan—their grandfather's alcoholism and early death, his father's divorce and accident. Tess, too, had lost her father at an early age, and her mother—Geneva's daughter—had inherited a weakness for drink. "Maybe that happiness will make a difference," Dev said. "Mellow you out."

"Like you, you mean?"

"Me?"

"Mr. Mellow." Tess nudged one of her sandals loose and dangled it over her brightly polished toes. "I'm surprised people don't check for a pulse when you stop moving. Look at you now, all nestled into that chair and ready for a nap."

"Sounds like a good idea." He smiled and closed his eyes. "I didn't have any plans for the rest of the afternoon. Except for getting some writing done."

"So why are you here?" She rustled some papers

and closed a drawer with a quiet thunk. "Not that I haven't enjoyed your company. And your compliments. But you're not going to get any writing done here."

"Maybe I'm looking for inspiration."

"And maybe you thought you'd find it around the corner."

Cove Street. Addie's place. His cousin always had been able to read him like a book. "I haven't been there yet."

"But you're thinking of going."

"Guilty as charged."

"And you came here looking for my blessing."

He opened his eyes and stared at her. "Do I need it?"

She'd slipped her sandal back on and tucked both feet beneath her desk. She regarded him like a prim schoolmarm, her hands folded on her neatened work space. "I don't like being caught in the middle, Dev."

He straightened and brought his elbows down on his knees, leaning forward. "What makes you think you are?"

"Don't be dense. I'm caught between you and Charlie, who's convinced you're the reason Addie broke up with Mick—who happens to be one of the nicest men she's ever met."

"Wait a min—"

"And between you and Addie," Tess continued, "who always tries so hard to keep the peace and always seems to end up getting trampled and left with nothing. And between you and Quinn, who happens to like you a lot but is worried about your intentions toward Addie, whom he absolutely adores, as do we all."

Tess sighed and shoved a hand through her hair.

"And I'll probably end up getting stuck between you and Rosie, since she's showing all the signs of developing a minor crush on you. And since I'd planned on asking you to help me out with supervising her this summer—if you actually stick around, that is. You name it, I'm stuck, right in the middle. And I don't like it." She slashed a hand through the air. "Not one bit."

"Wait a minute." Dev stood to pace a tight circle. He'd missed most of Tess's rant after that first blast: *Addie broke up with Mick.* The words had rammed through him like the iron ball on a wrecking crane.

"First," he said, "this so-called problem with Charlie is a nonstarter. She and I have never gotten along. And that has nothing to do with you."

"But everything to do with Addie." Tess relaxed against her desk. "Have you ever wondered why Charlie's always been so hard on you?"

"I figured it was a personality clash. Although I like her just fine." He gave Tess a quick grin. "Just don't tell her that."

Tess shook her head. "She's never liked the way you treat Addie."

"I was rotten to her—to them both, when we were kids, I know that. Teased them every chance I got. But that was a long time ago."

"And I always stuck up for you."

"You did?"

"Yep. Stuck in the middle, even back then."

Tess glanced at her watch and rose from her seat. "You're my cousin. I don't exactly have a large supply of relatives. And you're one that I actually like."

"That's nice to hear."

"Dev." She sighed again and moved to stand before

him. "There's a great deal to like about you. There always has been. I just wish you'd grow up and decide to like yourself, too."

He gazed over the top of her head and squinted at the wall, working his jaw to try to get the next words out. "I always thought you could see right through me. It would be nice to discover I've been right about that all these years."

She lifted a hand to his cheek. "You know I love you, don't you?"

"Yeah."

"Then you'll understand that what I'm about to say is going to hurt us both. A lot."

She lowered her hand and looked him straight in the eye. "I think you should stay away from Addie this summer. In spite of the fact that I think you'd make a very special couple if you'd—no," Tess said, frowning. "Now I'm arguing with myself, and there's not much middle ground there."

She stalked away, whirled back. "The thing is, I don't want to see Addie get trampled—again—when you leave. Even if you didn't mean to do it, you'd end up hurting her. And then I'd have to hurt you."

CHAPTER SEVEN

ADDIE STOOD ON THE expansive back terrace at
Chandler House on a beautiful Fourth of July afternoon, sipping Julia's perfectly sweetened lemonade.
She concentrated on the tickle of cool ocean breeze,
the extravagant perfume of Geneva's roses and the
peaks of the white tent pitched over the lawn. The
murmuring voices of the guests spoke of everything
and anything but the darkly handsome man prowling
the edges of the crowd at the bar.

She noticed the expensively dressed women who
occasionally stopped his restless pacing to engage him
in conversation. Old friends, old connections. Comfortable old habits in his comfortable old world.

"Don't you think?" Tess nudged Addie's arm.

"Hmm?"

"See?" Charlie made a beeline for one of the stone
benches set along the balustrade. "Addie's getting tired
of all this wedding talk, too."

"But this is the perfect chance to see how to
arrange things for the wedding reception." Tess
pointed at the scene below. "I'm not sure I'd put the
tent in the middle of the lawn. Making a space for a
dance floor under the stars would be better, don't
you think?"

"Who said anything about dancing?" Charlie sighed. "This whole thing is getting out of control."

Tess crossed her arms. "Only because you're not keeping up with developments."

"Maybe she should have more of a say in her own wedding." Addie squeezed in beside Charlie on the bench and dropped an arm over her shoulder. "Do you want to have dancing at your reception?"

"I don't know."

Addie sent Tess a brief warning look, silently begging her to keep her mouth shut. "Does Jack?"

"Probably."

"Wouldn't you like to dance with him on your wedding day?"

Charlie shrugged. "Maybe. Probably."

"Knowing Jack, I bet he'd love it." Addie smiled at both her friends. "And I think Tess's idea of dancing under the stars is romantic. And fun. Your guests would love it, too."

"I'm sorry." Tess leaned against the balustrade, beside Charlie. "I'm getting plans for your wedding mixed up with ideas for my own."

"Maybe you should consult more with Tess," Addie suggested. "You wouldn't want her to hog all the best ideas for herself."

Charlie narrowed her eyes at Addie. "You know, you may think you've got everyone fooled with your image as this sweet little do-gooder, but I can see through your act."

Addie donned her most useful wide-eyed, innocent expression. "I don't think I'm fooling people."

Tess frowned at something in the scene below and took a sip of her soft drink. "When are you and Maudie going to the city to pick up your gown?" she asked Charlie.

"Wednesday. In the middle of the week, in the middle of the busiest season of the year, for cryin' out loud. How much sense does that make?"

"Considering that you may have to find someone to make some last-minute alterations," Tess said, "it makes a lot of sense to get the dress as soon as possible."

"I can hardly wait to see it." Addie stood and stole a glance at the bar. "You are going to give us a sneak preview, right?"

"Yeah."

"Come on." Tess pulled Charlie to her feet. "Let's go inside and scout through the parlor and dining room. I want to make sure we have enough seating for the shower."

THE SIZE OF THE CROWD and the activities of the Fourth of July garden party should have been enough to keep Dev's radar from zeroing in on Addie, but it wasn't. He knew she'd watched the kids' sack races and sampled one of Julia's teriyaki chicken skewers. He noticed her chatting with Quinn and fussing over Toni Hulstrom's new baby. He was aware of the moment she'd left the terrace and disappeared into the house with Tess and Charlie.

He wondered what they were up to and how long they'd be up to it.

He'd managed to stay away from her for five days, but with every passing hour, his need to see her—to talk with her—increased. She was a part of this place, a part of his life here. And he missed her.

At one point he'd decided to wander past her and exchange a quick, casual greeting. If he didn't find a chance to talk to her before she left, she might assume he was avoiding her—and wouldn't that hurt her feelings? But one warning glance from Tess had sent him in another direction.

He stood near the horseshoes pit, pretending to watch the match underway and to listen to Karl Bern's theories on fish bait. Dev wondered if anything short of leaving Carnelian Cove would end his growing obsession with Addie, and that fact was ticking him off. He didn't want to leave, not until he'd made more progress with his writing. Not until he'd figured out where his story was headed. Or where his research might lead him.

He didn't want a lot of things, he told himself as Courtney Whitfield waved and sauntered his way, but they kept getting shoved in his face.

"Dev, you scoundrel." Courtney leaned in and angled her cheek against his in one of those near-miss kisses that set his teeth on edge. Her breath smelled of the margarita in her hand and her breasts pressed against his arm like pillows. "How nice it is to see you again after all these years."

"Is it?"

Courtney's features sharpened as she laughed off his comment. "It certainly is. Where have you been hiding all this time?"

"I haven't been hiding. You found me."

"So I did." She lifted her glass to her lips and delicately licked the salt encrusting the rim. "What have you been up to?"

"This and that."

"Ah. A man of mystery." Her smile widened, and she sipped her drink. "I love a good mystery, myself."

He gazed over the top of her head, scanning the crowd for Addie.

"Aren't you going to ask me what I've been up to?" Courtney moved to his side, facing the horseshoes game. Moved closer. "You might be surprised by the answer."

Dev ordered himself to be polite. For five minutes, anyway. "Surprise me, then."

"I'm divorced."

No surprise there.

"Four years, now. And I'm working in a dress shop—Lulu's, on Second Street." She paused for another sip. "Part-time, for now. I'm hoping to learn enough about the business to open my own."

He spared her a noncommital grunt and waited for the next bit of information.

"I never thought I'd run my own business," she said, turning to face him. "Did you?"

"I don't run a business."

She tilted her head to the side with one of her charming social laughs, the kind of perfectly pitched trill that sent chills up his spine. "Honestly, Dev, if I didn't know you better, I'd think you were going out of your way to tease me."

"Then it's a good thing you know me as well as you do." He caught a glimpse of Tess—and the daggers she was aiming his way—and wondered whether being polite was worth the trouble.

Where was Addie?

"We go way back, don't we, Dev?" Courtney raised an impossibly tanned hand flashing with polish and jewels to rearrange her lush black hair over her eyes. And then she let her hand fall, brushing her fingertips over his forearm in a touch that was casual, brief and loaded with meaning. "Further back than either of us would like to admit."

"I don't mind admitting how much distance I've put between myself and certain things."

Once again, annoyance flashed across her features before she regained her composure and poked out her lower lip in a pretty pout. "I hope that doesn't mean you're going to be in a hurry to leave us again. Jack Maguire said you'd be sticking around until the end of summer."

"That's right. Until after the wedding, anyway."

"I can't believe Charlie Keene is getting married. And to a man like Jack."

"Why not?"

"Well, she's…" Courtney's pout took on a nasty edge. "It's a surprise, that's all. She never seemed the marrying type."

"Jack's lucky she waited for him."

"Oh, yes," Courtney said, dripping with generosity. "I'm sure they'll both be very happy."

Courtney flexed one of her ankles, swiveling her foot on the heel of her silvery sandal and passing her polished toes over the tip of his shoe. "Are you going to the anniversary dance at the club?"

"I hadn't thought about it." There was Addie—over by the barbecue, chatting with Ben Chandler and Maudie Keene. And sparing him the occasional glance with one of her shuttered I'm-ticked-but-I-don't-want-to-show-it expressions.

"You should." Courtney leaned in, whisper close,

keeping things confidential. Intimate. "I'm on the events committee this year, and I can assure you it's going to be a fabulous evening."

"Hmm."

"You're still a member, aren't you?"

"I have no idea." Still watching Addie, Dev caught the flicker of misery in her eyes as she stole a glance at Courtney. Addie waved goodbye to Ben and Maudie and headed up the hill, toward the house.

The hell with avoiding Addie, thought Dev. The hell with them all—Tess, and Charlie, and Geneva and Lena and everyone. The hell with his conscience, too.

"Well, if you've let your membership lapse," Courtney said, "I could—"

"Thanks. Here." Dev pulled her glass from her hands. "Let me get you another one of these."

"Aren't you a sweetheart?" She slipped her hand through his arm as he led the way across the lawn and toward the bar. "You've always been a perfect gentleman."

But Courtney's sticky lie about his manners wasn't a strong enough adhesive to keep him by her side. While she gave her order to the bartender, Dev made his escape.

AFTER A QUICK TRIP to the powder room to lock herself away from the crowd for a few minutes and splash some water on her face, Addie wandered through Chandler House. She paused in the doorway of the morning room, where Tess had dragged Charlie for one more consultation on wedding-shower décor. Addie leaned a shoulder against the jamb, trying to picture Charlie enjoying her party. Instead, she remembered

Courtney Whitfield stroking her blood-red nails down Dev's sleeve.

Addie checked her watch. Hours remained until the fireworks would start, but she doubted she'd stay for the celebration. Coming here had been a mistake; leaving early would fix it.

She decided on a detour to the entry hall to study the two undamaged windows. And as she climbed the stairs, the end-of-day sunlight seemed to make the wavy glass shimmer and her troubles ease.

Cool marble steps, warm wood tones, plush carpet, hushed echoes—she'd once loved pulling the feel of Chandler House around her like an elegant ball gown. Now she paused on the landing to brush a fingertip along smooth veins of lead. Topaz and emerald, sapphire and ruby—her private collection of precious gems. She'd need all her skill to make the repairs to the missing windows, to make the new pieces seem as though they'd always been part of the picture.

A part of the picture. Seeing Courtney Whitfield flirting with Dev had reminded Addie she'd never have a real place in his world.

She stared at her hand as she drew it from the window—short, naked nails and a bandage wrapped around yesterday's nick. She glanced at her thin cotton blouse, plain linen pants and simple sandals—inexpensive basics from a local discount store. She ran her fingers through her serviceable ponytail and tried to remember the last time she'd had the ends trimmed.

No wonder Dev hadn't been back to her shop in a week.

With a sigh, she turned to leave. And found Dev slouched against the wall at the foot of the stairs, one long leg stretched over the bottom tread, barring her path.

She hesitated, squeezing the handrail, and then continued to descend. Surely good manners would force him to shift out of her way. But as she neared the spot where he sat, motionless, she remembered Dev had never been one to let manners dictate his behavior.

"Are you going to let me pass?" she asked.

"Eventually."

She was tempted to wait him out, but after a few seconds she grew impatient. "What do you want?"

"Now there's a dangerous question." He looked up at her, and his bland expression gave no clue to his intentions or emotions as he patted the tread beside him. "Have a seat, and I'll think of a decent answer."

A few minutes ago, the silence in the house had felt welcoming and secure. Now it seemed to close in on her like a trap. "I should go back outside."

"Is someone waiting for you out there?"

She recognized the faint trace of pain beneath the sarcastic challenge of his tone. It reminded her of a lonely boy left to entertain himself. A sensitive boy trapped at the center of family battles. Rather than answer, she slowly lowered herself to a tread above him. "There's more comfortable seating in other rooms."

"I'm sure there are hundreds of comfortable chairs in dozens of rooms." He bent the leg that had blocked her way, resting his hand over his raised knee. "But this is more private."

"Do we need privacy?"

He didn't answer, and after some time had passed, she realized he'd chosen to ignore her question.

Uneasy with his brooding silence, she searched for a way to fill it. "What would you like to discuss?"

"I'm not in the mood for a discussion. Or an interview." His lips thinned in a scowl. "I just wanted to talk with you. It's been a while."

"Yes, it has. Nearly a week. But I suppose you've been busy." She regretted her words as soon as they'd escaped. Hadn't she just been thinking he had no good reason to seek out her company? "Sorry."

"That always was a bad habit of yours. Apologizing," he added when she gave him a quizzical look.

"I'm only being polite," she said primly.

"Spreading a layer of snotty attitude over things isn't an improvement on the automatic-apology routine, but I think I like it better."

"And comments like that would explain why it's been a while since our last conversation." She reached for the handrail, intending to pull herself up and step right over him.

"Wait." He grabbed her wrist. They both froze. And then his fingers tightened and his thumb brushed across the sensitive spot inside her wrist in what might have been a tentative caress before he released her.

Had it been a caress?

"We don't need to go through the motions with the small talk," he said. "Do we?"

She forced herself to relax. She didn't want him to see that his opinion mattered. Or that the way he'd sought out her company meant so much. Far, far too much. She'd wasted years waiting for these things, years craving his attention—his touch. She'd spent years resenting him—and berating herself—for it all.

He was right—the two of them were years beyond

the small-talk phase. "No," she told him, settling back into her narrow seat. "We don't."

"Good." He tipped his head to rest against the wall and shut his eyes. "I ran out of social conversation about an hour ago."

She stared at the black lashes fanning over his tanned cheeks. Such ridiculously long, nearly feminine lashes, an amusing contrast to a stern, masculine landscape.

"About those apologies," he said. "They're not about being polite. Not really." He opened his eyes and rolled his head against the wall to face her. "Are they?"

"Why are you bothering to ask me?" She flapped a hand at him. "It's your theory."

"And topic number one bites the dust."

Her lips twitched as she suppressed a smile.

"Okay," Dev said. "Topic number two. Let's try things we have in common—plenty of those. A memory. Remember Bud Soames?"

"Your partner in crime."

"A few." He flicked a glance at her from beneath those dark lashes. "There weren't as many crimes as people seem to think."

"Memory is a tricky thing."

"Yeah." He frowned. "Makes me think I used to like living here."

"Didn't you?" Addie leaned forward. "Ever?"

She told herself it was only her imagination that his features softened as he stared at her. And that she could see the hint of a wistful smile in his eyes. Because whatever she thought she'd found, it disappeared a few seconds later.

He looked away, toward the massive entry doors. "I didn't have a choice, did I?"

"Kids don't. That's one of the things that makes them kids."

"Do adults have any more choices, I wonder?"

"Is that what you were doing, sitting in here all by yourself?" She traced a pattern on the carpet. "Contemplating your choices in life?"

"I don't need to go off somewhere by myself to do that." He studied her again with that odd intensity, as if trying to look deep beneath her skin to her very core. "Where do you go to do your thinking?" he asked.

Her finger moved around the edge of a fanciful curling vine. "I don't spend a lot of time doing that kind of thinking. I'm too busy working, most of the time."

"Ah, yes. Your shop."

She searched for a trace of sarcasm in his tone before she caught herself falling into the old, defensive patterns. Dev wasn't judging or teasing. And he had seemed genuinely interested in her business last week when he'd stopped by.

"I don't mind working so hard," she said. "I love making pictures with glass. When I took my first stained-glass class, something fell into place for me. Like the way glass pieces click into place when they've been ground to fit."

She wrapped her arms around her knees. "Someone once told me that if you can find a way to make a living doing the thing that makes you happy, you'll have a happy life."

His brows drew together. "Now there's something to think about."

"What about your writing?" she asked.

"What about it?"

"Does it make you happy?"

"Sometimes. But I wouldn't count on it making me a living."

"I remember the story you wrote about the old lighthouse on the point," she said. "The one that won that award—what was that? The award from *The Cove Press*. I loved that story," she added when he didn't respond. "Would you show me another of your stories someday?"

"Yes," he said after a long pause. "If you'd like."

The tall case clock in the study bonged the hour, and someone in a distant room laughed. A slice of ruby-red light slid over the back of her hand like a wound, and she turned up her palm and curled her fist to capture it inside.

They should go. She wanted to stay.

"What were you going to tell me about Bud Soames?" she asked.

"I've been remembering a day when we were both seniors. I was in my car, out in the student lot, moving toward the exit. And then I saw you."

He stared at the hall as if he was gazing into the past. "You were standing on that strip of grass between the lot and the street, holding a big stack of books. And you were watching me."

She remembered that day. It seemed she could recall any day that had included Dev. She nodded, even though she knew he couldn't see her, and waited for him to start again.

"I was going to stop beside you. I had my hand on the button to lower the window and ask if you wanted a ride home." He turned to face her. "I wanted to talk with you."

"What would you have said?"

One side of his mouth twisted in a half grin. "There's another habit of yours—always cutting right to the heart of the matter. Why waste time on small talk when you can skip ahead to the tough questions?" His smile faded. "Why are you so tough on me, Addie?"

CHAPTER EIGHT

ADDIE RESTED HER CHIN on her knees. There were so many answers she could give to Dev's question, but it would be easier to invent one. Easier on herself, perhaps, but unfair to Dev. "Maybe I'm trying to level the playing field," she said at last.

He sighed and shook his head. "I wish you didn't feel at such a disadvantage."

Disadvantage. Sitting here with him, like this, it seemed odd to consider the advantages she'd had over this handsome, wealthy, talented man. She'd had a mother who loved and sacrificed for her child, for one. "I'm not sure 'disadvantage' is the right word," she said.

"Maybe not." He paused and rubbed his hand over his knee. "On that day—that day Bud climbed into my car—I wanted to talk with you like *this*. The way we're talking now."

In her imagination, she was back on that soft, grassy strip again, watching him drive toward her. The books were heavy, the edges of the binding biting into her arms as a tickling bead of sweat moved down her spine. Panic mixed with anticipation as she realized he was looking her way, slowing his car.

What would she have said if he'd offered her a ride? What would they have talked about if she'd accepted?

"We were too young to have the kind of conversation we're having now."

"Maybe." He gave her a searing, unsettling look. A look that started the slow, heavy beat of awareness pulsing through her system. She wished she could control her reaction to him.

She wished she could make him react the same way to her. Tempt him to lean close, to brush his lips over hers, to whisper her name, to take her in his arms...

Someone walked by, heels clicking swiftly down the rear hallway near Geneva's office, speaking in the halting, one-sided bursts of a cell-phone conversation.

"I should go back to the party," she said.

"So should I."

But Dev didn't move, and he didn't look away.

Addie straightened and folded her hands in her lap. "Tell me what you were going to say about Bud."

"Oh, yeah." Dev frowned and glanced away. "He caught up to me, since my car was moving so slowly. And he pulled the door open and jumped into the passenger seat, just like he belonged there. Which he did, because he was my friend."

Dev lowered his hand to the carpet, his fingers resting a fraction of an inch from the toe of her sandal. "Then you dropped your books, and Bud laughed and pointed at you. He said, 'What a loser.' I laughed, too, because that's what I did—what everyone expected of me. But inside of me, this other voice was telling me that I was the loser. Not because I'd laughed at you, but because I let Bud into my car instead of you. Because we never got to have that talk."

Dev shifted to face her. "I can't make up for what happened before. And I'm not sure we can ever be friends. But I'd like to try. I'd like to have a friendship with you, Addie. I came in here looking for that today."

He stood and reached for her hand, his palm upturned, offering to help her rise from her seat on the stairs. "Do you think we could at least pretend to be friends?" he asked. "For old times' sake?"

"I don't think that would be too hard." She cocked her head to one side. "But did we ever at least pretend to like each other?"

"Good point." His smile tugged up at one corner in a more familiar tilt. "That part could be an exciting new element in our pseudo-relationship."

He leaned in close, took her by the arms and hauled her to her feet. Tipping her off her step, off balance, until she fell against his chest. The stunning contact nearly knocked her senseless.

He held her there for a second longer than necessary. An extra second in which she sensed his tension and absorbed his heat. The slight parting of his lips, the sharp intake of his breath, the intense yearning in his gaze.

"Addie," he whispered as he tilted his head toward hers.

A door slammed nearby, and laughter blasted through the hall. Dev released her and stepped back, out of her way.

She moved to the entry floor and headed toward the back of the house, Dev beside her. Close beside her. She imagined she could still feel his heat. "I was thinking about leaving the party earlier," she told him. "Before our visit."

"I wish you wouldn't go just yet." He caught her wrist again, stopping her, and she didn't have to use her imagination. His fingers stayed closed over her skin, warm and secure. And this time she didn't mistake the simmer in his stare. "I'd like you to stay," he said. "We could pretend to ignore each other."

"Sounds like a plan."

"Okay, then." He closed his hand over hers and gave it a soft squeeze before letting her go. "I'll take what I can get."

EARLY THE FOLLOWING MORNING, Dev lifted Geneva's bags into the trunk of her long, luxurious sedan and waited for his grandmother to make her farewells to her whining herd of Yorkies. He'd promised to take care of the dogs' daily walk, but he'd been careful to avoid promising that he'd be the one on the other end of the leashes. Rosie, Quinn and Tess had driven a hard bargain, but he figured fifty dollars for the kid and a few afternoons spent keeping an eye on her for his cousin was worth escaping two weeks of poop-scoop duty.

"Don't forget to close the gate after Julia leaves this evening," Geneva said as she settled in the passenger seat for the trip to the Cove's miniature airport.

"I won't." He gently closed her door and circled to the driver's side.

"And don't forget to collect the paper each day from the bottom of the drive," she added as he climbed in. "They won't fit in the box if you let them pile up."

"I've got everything written down." He pulled away and headed down the hill. "I can handle it. I'm a big boy now."

"I'm aware of that fact." Geneva gave him a considering look. "And so, it seems, are several women in Carnelian Cove."

"Not several." Dev shot her a pained look. "And shouldn't this subject be off-limits for a guy's grandmother?"

"It's not a subject. It's an observation."

He'd thought one extra-large cup of coffee would be enough to sharpen his wits and get him through this errand without getting his butt kicked by his grandmother. He'd been wrong. "Any woman who might be aware of my presence in the Cove should also be aware that I'm not interested. I don't live here. I don't intend to stick around for long. And I don't plan on seeing anyone while I'm here."

"Hmm."

"What?"

"I said, 'Hmm.'"

"And what does that 'hmm' mean, exactly?"

"Addie Sutton."

Dev clamped his lips together. He'd relived those moments on the stairs last evening a hundred times. But they still felt new, fresh and fragile and his alone.

His and Addie's.

"You told me to stay away from her," he said at last.

"You were seventeen at the time. And inclined to disobedience if you deemed the punishment worth the effort."

"Then maybe I never thought she was worth it."

"Hmm."

They rode in silence for several minutes. Minutes that poked at Dev until he could feel the lumpy bruises on his conscience. "She wasn't worth it," he told his grandmother.

"So you say."

"That's right. That's what I'm saying."

"The question is, do you still believe it?"

"Now?" He straightened his fingers and slowly wrapped them more tightly around the steering wheel. "I'm not sure what to think. Or to believe."

Having Tess warning him to avoid Addie and Geneva shoving him in her direction didn't help the situation.

Geneva pointed at a tall, green Victorian house as they passed. "Stan Waterman's son was accepted at West Point."

"Dave Waterman? That scrawny little kid with the white hair? The one with all those rabbits that won ribbons at the fair every summer?"

"He was the starting center fielder on the high school baseball team last year," Geneva said. "He'll be leaving for New York soon."

"Hard to imagine." On the surface, the Cove seemed the same old place. But things changed. People changed. Maybe Addie had changed, too, in ways he couldn't see.

"What about the rabbits?" he asked.

Geneva gave him one of her exasperated looks, but she couldn't quite hide the laughter in her eyes. "I doubt Dave is taking them with him to West Point."

"What about Jim Franks?" Dev asked. He'd once thought his grandmother had a soft spot for the elegant widower. "Is he still around?"

"Jim died last year." Geneva laced her fingers together on her lap. "He'd remarried, shortly before he got sick. His widow, Sophie, is on the board at The Breakers."

Dev turned onto the highway and headed north. Soon the tiny airport, perched on a bluff overlooking

Elkhorn Beach, came into view. A bright-orange Coast Guard helicopter swooped in from the west and disappeared behind a line of tall, twisted cypress.

"Speaking of The Breakers," Geneva said.

"Were we?"

"Will you be going to the anniversary dance?"

"I hadn't thought about it."

"I saw you speaking with that Whitfield woman yesterday." Geneva's lips thinned in a disapproving line. "I'm sure the subject of the dance came up."

"Courtney. She mentioned she's on some sort of club committee."

"I doubt that's all she had to say on the subject."

He exited the highway and began the climb toward the airport parking area. Since he couldn't think of a way to respond to Geneva's comment without launching into a topic he didn't want to discuss with her, he said nothing.

"She asked you to escort her, didn't she?"

"Why the interrogation?" Dev punched the big metal button and yanked the parking ticket from the machine at the gate. "You're not in charge of my social life. Not anymore."

"I was never in charge." She pointed to an empty space beneath a tall tree. "If I had been, I would have chosen a different set of friends for you."

Dev switched off the ignition and settled back against the seat. "Maybe you should have."

"You wouldn't have listened."

"I'm listening now."

"Yes, you are. You have been listening this summer. I don't know whether to be grateful or concerned." Geneva glanced at her watch and then back at him. "I think we have time for a drink in the lounge before I have to go through security. We could find a quiet spot to continue this discussion."

"It can wait. Don't worry," he said, grinning, "I promise I'll still be listening when you get back."

He stared ahead, watching distant waves crest in white ridges and crash to foam along the shore. On the horizon, a string of boats marked the edge of a fishing ground. "There's something more important I want to discuss right now."

"Your father's papers."

His grandmother had always possessed an uncanny ability to guess what was on his mind. "Where are they?"

"I don't suppose there's any point in refusing to answer that question, since you'll likely turn my house inside out looking for them in my absence."

"This trip of yours does give me an excellent opportunity to do some quality ransacking."

"Sorry to spoil your fun, but I left the key to the family files where you'll easily find it. In the top right drawer of my desk."

"Well." Dev tapped his fingers on the steering wheel. "That was easy."

"You haven't yet seen the files." Geneva's lips turned up in a sly smile. "Everything is in order, but there's a great deal of it."

"And it just so happens I have a great deal of time on my hands this summer."

He exited the car and jogged to the passenger side to open his grandmother's door. She followed him to the rear of the car and waited as he hauled her suitcases from the trunk.

"Julia left a few dishes for you in the freezer," she said.

Geneva's cook was taking a holiday, too. "She didn't have to do that," Dev said, "but I'm glad she did."

"Please leave her kitchen tidy, if you use it."

"I know how to clean up after myself."

"I wish I could take credit for that," his grandmother said, "but it must be a habit you developed after you left home."

"Amazing what the sudden absence of a maid and a cook will do for a guy."

He closed the trunk, stacked the cases and fell into step beside Geneva as she walked toward the terminal entrance. "Say hi to Aunt Jacqueline for me," he said. "And have fun on your cruise."

"Leaving me with a list of things to do?" She walked through the sliding doors and turned to take her bags from him. "Wait for me here, if you don't mind."

Dev nodded and strolled toward a compact lounge area a few feet away. A twenty-minute drive to the airport, dozens of parking slots within a few yards of the door, a nonexistent line at the check-in counter— this small-town airport routine was a nice change from the big-city hassles.

Geneva returned a minute later, her boarding pass in hand. "I won't keep you long."

"I don't mind waiting."

"That's right," she said as she tucked her ticket into a purse pocket. "You have all summer."

"What did you want to tell me?"

"I wanted to remind you that you're not seventeen anymore." She stepped in close to press her cheek against his in one of her formal displays of affection. "I hope you don't take the entire summer to realize that fact."

YOU'RE NOT SEVENTEEN ANYMORE.

Geneva's words lodged in his brain like a catchy but obnoxious advertising jingle, annoying him as he sped down the highway, heading back to Carnelian Cove.

Okay, so he wasn't seventeen. He knew that. But damn, every second he spent in Addie's presence made him feel as though he were stuck in some sort of time warp. Awkward. Insecure. Hormonal. Out of control.

There had to be some way to snap out of it.

Why did he care about her so much, anyway? It wasn't as if he wanted to date her. Get her in bed, yes—that's what any normal, healthy heterosexual male wanted to do with an appealing, single female. But with Addie, the normal-and-healthy routine would never be as straightforward as it should be.

She'd always held some strange and powerful fascination for him.

Which explained all the boundaries Lena and Geneva had erected to keep him away from her.

And now, just when Geneva had given him the green light, Tess had issued her own warning to stay away from her friend.

Friendship. What a bunch of bullshit. What an idiotic tactic he'd tried the day before. Tess's fault— that's what that had been. Trying to get around his cousin's embargo by promising to play nice with Addie all summer.

He and Addie were already as friendly as they were ever going to get. Their problem was all that history getting in their way. All those family expectations and mixed signals to sort through. All that seventeen-year-old hormonal crap, warping the here and now.

And he was back to square one. Damn.

So what did he want—besides getting her in bed? And why did it have to be Addie between the sheets, anyway? There were plenty of other attractive, willing women. Courtney Whitfield, for one.

He winced.

Okay, back to Addie. He always seemed to circle back to her, even when he thought he was heading in a straight line to somewhere else. That had to mean something—although what that something was, he'd never been able to figure out. But he sure was getting tired of feeling like some rodent running on a squeaky wheel.

He rubbed a hand over his chest. There they were again—those gnawing, rodentlike doubts. It was time—well past time—to quit acting like a confused seventeen-year-old and take a man's chances. He turned down Cove Street and headed toward A Slice of Light.

No need to blow it, though, he thought as he passed her shop and made the first turn in a trip around the block. He needed a strategy. Slow and steady would probably work in this situation. Let her know he was interested, gauge her reaction, build her trust, take some easy steps before the first move.

Okay, then.

He pulled to the curb near her shop, exited his car and stepped off the squeaky wheel.

CHAPTER NINE

ADDIE SLID HER GUIDE into place at the long edge of a
large rectangle of glass and ran her cutter up the center.
A quick pinch with the running pliers at the base of the
pale, hair-thin score neatly separated the piece into
two squares. She carefully added the new pieces to the
stack on her right, brushed her work surface to remove
any tiny chips of glass—like the one that had nicked
her left palm earlier that morning—and then lifted the
next piece into position.

And then she paused, as she'd done a dozen times
this morning, to relive the ridiculously giddy, chest-
tightening, heart-racing, thought-scrambling thrill of
Dev's almost-a-kiss on the stairs in Chandler House.

He'd nearly kissed her. Almost. She was sure of it.
And because it had only been almost-a-kiss, she'd been
free to complete the details in one fantasy after another.

And to stash those details beside the details of all
the other Dev-related fantasies she'd indulged in over
the past twenty-five years.

Her shop door opened, and the object of those fantasies walked through it. "Hi, Dev."

"Hi, Addie." He paused by the door and slid his
hands into his pockets. "Aren't you going to ask me
what I'm doing here?"

"I wouldn't want to be predictable."

She repositioned the guide and pressed the cutter against the edge of the glass with trembling fingers. It slipped off and smacked down against the table, taking with it a tiny pile of glass shards. Frowning, she made a second try to catch the edge, and this time the cutter began a smooth glide up the glass with that paper-ripping sound that told her the score was deep and even. "So, what are you doing here?" she asked.

"Just dropped by to see how you're doing."

Of course. That's the kind of things friends—or people pretending to be friends—did. She could handle that. No reason at all for her pulse to race and her breath to catch as he moved closer. "I'm fine," she said. "And you?"

"Fine."

"I'm glad to hear it."

His eyes crinkled with amusement—probably at their oddly formal exchange—and her face warmed. It was going to take a while to get used to this friend-ship thing.

And maybe she couldn't handle a friendship with Dev Chandler after all.

Too bad she couldn't afford to take a vacation. With Dev in Carnelian Cove for the next several weeks, this would be a good time to get out of town.

He watched her turn the long rectangle of glass and straighten it for another cut. "I just dropped Geneva at the airport."

"Tess said she's going on a cruise."

"That's right."

Addie made another cut, split the halves and stacked the two new squares on the others.

"What are you doing?" he asked.

"A glass shipment arrived." She lifted another large piece, and he grabbed one side to help her lower it to the table. "These pieces are too large to sell to crafters," she told him, "so unless someone asks for a piece of this size, I cut them down to make them more portable."

He watched as she scored another line. "You're not cutting it all the way through."

"No." She set the cutter aside and picked up her pliers. "It's that molecules thing again."

"Ah, yes. The molecular mysteries of lead. And glass." His mouth curved in a wry smile. "All to be revealed at some other time."

"I'd say I'm sorry for the way I behaved when you came in last week," she said, "but someone told me I'm not supposed to do that anymore."

"Not supposed to do what—behave obnoxiously?"

"Apologize. And I wasn't obnoxious."

"You were horrible. Disgusting." He placed a hand over his heart. "I'm considering therapy to help me recover from the trauma."

She smiled at his teasing, and then she realized she'd been teasing, too. They'd been flirting. Sort of.

But Dev didn't flirt. Not with her, especially. Whatever this was, though, it felt comfortable. Pleasant.

Friendly.

"You were saying?" he asked.

"Hmm?"

"About those molecules…"

"Oh." She glanced at the pliers in her hand, searching for her place in the conversation. "Yes. Well. Glass isn't a crystal—its molecules don't line up in a pattern.

That's why you can cut it in curves. All you need to do to break glass is to decrease its strength along the line of a score, and the molecules beneath that line will separate when you apply a bit of pressure. Here," she said as she handed him the pliers. "You give it a try."

She helped him place the curved end of the running pliers over one edge of the score she'd made and told him to squeeze gently. The glass separated into two neat halves with a whisper of a snap.

"Cool," he said.

"I think so."

He glanced at the pieces displayed in her window. "You cut all those pieces just like that?"

"Not exactly like that, but yeah, it's the same basic idea."

He watched her make another couple of breaks and then wandered off to stroll slowly through one of her narrow shop aisles, studying the tools hanging from hooks and spread over various shelves. "Farrier nails?" He lifted a packet of a dozen enclosed in a small, clear plastic bag. "Aren't farriers the people who shoe horses?"

"Yes. But I use the nails to hold the caming—the lead—in place while I'm assembling a design."

He replaced the little bag. "Geneva's going to visit with Tess's mother for a couple of days in the city before heading down to the Caribbean."

"Sounds nice." Addie couldn't picture his grandmother lounging on a deck chair. Geneva never seemed to lounge anywhere. "Where is the ship stopping?"

"A couple of ports in the Caribbean. What the hell is this for?" Dev lifted a curved and pointed piece of plastic.

Addie set aside the last of her glass squares and

wandered over to join him. "That's called a fid. A handy tool, really. It can do all sorts of things. Press foil over the edges of glass pieces, widen caming…"

He dropped the fid back into its box and continued down the aisle. "Cutters…groziers…pliers…putty…" He stopped and stared at an assortment of fine, sharp metal picks. "And here we have the handy instruments of torture."

Her shop door's bell jingled as a young couple entered. "Excuse me," she said, moving past Dev.

"No problem. I'm not going anywhere."

She greeted her customers—please, let them be customers—and felt Dev's gaze like a brand along her spine.

I'm not going anywhere. She couldn't decide whether his words were a promise or a threat.

If only they were true.

DEV STROLLED TOWARD the front of Addie's shop, closer to the large windows fronting Cove Street, where her stained-glass art was hung to tempt passersby. Nearby, a case displayed several glossy, oversize how-to-do-it paperbacks. He picked up a book with a simple mosaic on the cover and flipped through the pages, eavesdropping without appearing to do so.

"Is this locally made?" asked the woman, pointing to the stained-glass shop address hanging over the door.

Addie nodded. "All the pieces you see have been made here, in this shop."

"Are they all for sale?" asked the man. "I like this one."

Dev looked up to see him gesture toward a large

panel featuring a peacock perched on a stylized branch, its tail cascading in rich blues and greens. The clear glass surrounding the bird was broken by twiglike streaks of lead, making the structure of the glasswork part of the design. "Where did you get the idea for this?" the customer asked. "Did it come from a picture?"

"Not that one," Addie told him. "It's my own design."

And it was beautiful, Dev had to admit, now that he'd begun to notice things in Addie's shop other than its owner. Clever, imaginative. Much more interesting than the designs he saw in the pages of the book he was holding. Addie had always had a talent for drawing.

And she'd used her creative talents to develop her own business, something most people never accomplished.

"These lilies are beautiful." The woman bent to admire a large, square window with milky, pink glass flowers arching over neat squares of clear leaded glass. "Did you design this, too?"

"Yes." Addie explained the different kinds of glass she'd chosen to create the flowers and how some of the pieces had been reversed to add texture. She led the way to the storage bins on one wall and pulled out several pieces of the same milky glass—opalescent, she called it—and invited her customers to hold the pieces up to the light pouring through her shop windows so they could admire the effects.

"We've been thinking of having a window made for our place," the woman said. "But I wanted something with clearer glass than this."

Addie slid a piece of the opalescent glass back into its slot. "What's the style of your house?"

Dev listened as Addie discussed some interesting bits of glass history, helping the couple make a decision about a design that would satisfy their personal preferences while working with the design of their home.

Smart lady.

Next she pulled several squares of clear glass from her bins, explaining the manufacturing process that created different textures. The man seemed fascinated by the details and choices; the woman lifted each piece and looked through it, toward the light from the street. It was obvious they were enjoying their shopping experience.

Addie was a smooth saleswoman. While she shared her enthusiasm for her craft, she learned the man's grandmother had lived in a house with a stained-glass window and that the woman had a fondness for the same flowers she grew in her garden. Before fifteen minutes had passed, Addie had sold them the lilies and taken an order—and accepted a down payment— for two similar panels.

After making delivery plans, she walked the couple to the door, where she chatted with them for several more minutes, telling them how to get to one of the locals' favorite off-the-beaten-path beaches.

"You're good at this," Dev said once she'd closed the door behind her customers.

"Yes. I am." Her dimpled smile spread, wide and delighted, beneath the calculating gleam in her eyes. "And I just made a deal for a project that's going to keep me busy until I start on Tess's windows for Tidewaters."

"I never figured you for a businesswoman. I didn't mean that as an insult," he added when her smile dimmed. "I meant, I never pictured you running a shop."

"I doubt you thought of me at all."

He wanted to deny it, but he wouldn't lie to her. "That might explain it."

She moved past him and began sliding her glass samples back into their proper slots.

He stepped beside her and leaned in close. "Want to try to sell me something?" he asked.

She stiffened. "You didn't come in here to shop."

"No. I didn't." He fingered a strand of her hair and toyed with the ends that curled around his knuckle. "But I could be persuaded to change my mind."

When he heard the tiny catch in her breath, he held his, too. Her lashes fluttered as her gaze lowered to his hand. He let her silky hair slip over his fingers and then dropped his hand to his side, his pulse pounding through his body. This slow-and-steady routine was rough on a guy's blood pressure.

"Are you thinking of taking up mosaics as a hobby?" She turned, shifting a few inches away, and pointed to the book he still held. "It can be an easy one."

"Easy enough for a ten-year-old?"

"Easy enough for Rosie." Addie folded her arms and leaned against her sample display table, out of reach. "Is she still driving Tess nuts?"

Dev tossed the book on the table beside Addie. "She did this past week. Next week she'll be driving me nuts."

"You could get her set up with a mosaics project." Addie crossed the floor to select another book from her collection and thumbed through the pages. "A paving stone would be a nice gift. Personal. Handmade. Unique."

"How long does it take to make?" Dev followed her to examine the picture Addie showed him. "Okay, yeah, you're right—nice. Would that one take a week to make?"

Addie's husky laugh scraped along his skin, pricking hot-blooded goose bumps. He cleared his throat. "How about an afternoon?"

"That's more likely." She flipped to another page and showed him a picture of a butterfly done in a rainbow of colors. "You don't want to give her something too difficult at first. If she enjoys the activity, she'll want to do another one."

And buy more supplies to do it with. Sensible with her customers, smart with her business. Hard to say no to Addie Sutton.

"Sounds like a plan," Dev said as he took the book from her. "Okay, start selling me stuff."

"Don't you want to bring Rosie in and let her choose her supplies for herself?"

"Would that take an afternoon?"

There was that laugh again, coasting along his nerve endings like a drug. "Part of one, anyway." Addie tucked a bit of hair behind her ear. "You could fill the rest with a stop for an ice cream sundae and a walk along Shipwreck Beach to see if any of the surfers get bitten by a shark."

"Bloodthirsty, aren't you?"

"This is Rosie we're talking about."

"Yeah. Right." Dev grinned. "She'd love the shark angle."

"She'll love the mosaic idea, too." Addie gently pried the book from hands. "Tell you what. I'll sell you this book today, and you can discuss things with Rosie. If she thinks she'd like to give it a try, bring her by, and I'll set her up."

"Deal."

He followed Addie to her counter. While she wrote up the sale, he grabbed one of the flyers on the counter beside her. It was an advertisement for a stained-glass course. Four classes—the first starting this week.

Four chances to watch Addie in action. Four opportunities to move in closer, closer…

He held up the flyer. "I'm thinking this might be an interesting way to spend part of my summer vacation."

Addie looked at the paper in his hand and froze, as a series of emotions—dismay, annoyance, resignation, anticipation—dashed across her features.

Anticipation—yes, he'd definitely caught that.

"Well," she said at last.

"Well?"

"Well…yes." She slipped his book and receipt into a pretty paper bag. "It is interesting. I think so, anyway."

She handed him his purchase with one of her guileless, sidetracking smiles. "Thanks for stopping by. Let me know what Rosie decides."

He set the bag aside and leaned an elbow on the counter, bringing his face within a few tantalizing inches of hers. "And what about me?"

"You?"

He dropped his gaze to her mouth—to those beautiful, curving, plump, inviting lips—and then lifted it to meet hers again. "Wouldn't you like to know what I've decided?"

"That depends." She narrowed her eyes. "Have you decided you don't want to pretend to be friends anymore?"

Smart lady, all right.

CHAPTER TEN

ADDIE HAD THOUGHT SHE was well-prepared for her first stained-glass class. She'd arranged a roomy new work space, including a sturdy table and a couple of old metal stools she'd located in a secondhand shop. She'd assembled a basic supply kit for each of her students and selected a few simple patterns in a variety of styles.

But when Dev walked into her shop, Rosie in tow, her thoughts tumbled and tangled, and all her lesson plans seemed to bounce right out the door that clicked shut behind him.

He paused, shipped his hands into his pockets and smiled at her as if he could read her thoughts. As if he knew the effect he had on her. As if—

"Do you have anything in a slightly softer green?" Barb Katz refocused Addie's attention on the task at hand: helping her students find the pieces of glass they'd need to complete the patterns they'd chosen.

"There might be an opalescent piece that would work," Addie suggested.

"I don't care for those." Barb returned the square with a sigh. "They're so hard to see through."

"I think they're gorgeous." Teddi Moreno set a piece with wavy stripes like melting tropical sherbet over the others in her pile. "And each one is unique."

"Hi, Addie." Rosie leaned against the sample table, bouncing on the toes of her grubby athletic shoes. Up, down, up, down, emanating energy while sapping Addie's. "Dev told me I could pick everything out. Where's the stuff?"

"First you need a pattern." Addie pointed toward the rear of her shop. "Go help Dev choose one, and then you can start shopping for your glass."

"Cool." Rosie dashed off.

"Do you think my wife will like these?" Virgil Hawley, Addie's former high school algebra teacher, set two squares of rose-colored glass on the table. "She likes pink."

"I think she'll like whatever you choose for her," Addie told him.

Virgil frowned. "She didn't like the last present I gave her."

"What was that?" Teddi asked.

"A leaf blower."

Rosie materialized by Addie's side. "Here. This is the one we want." She waved a line drawing of a sunset over ocean swells. "I get to choose the glass. I'm Dev's assistant."

Addie turned to find him standing behind her, unnervingly close. His mouth eased into another of those casually intimate grins, the ones that seemed to brush like invisible fingertips over every inch of her skin.

"Hi, Addie."

"Hi, Dev."

"I think we should pick the sun piece first." Rosie pointed to a bin filled with yellow and orange glass squares. "Pull out a couple of those."

"Yes, ma'am."

He stepped around the table to follow Rosie's orders while Addie helped the other students finalize their selections. For the next several minutes she kept busy filling out receipts for more glass sales than she'd made in nearly a month.

At last it was Dev's turn to pay for his supplies. He and Rosie had chosen a nice mix of shimmery blue and green textured glasses for the water and found a stunning—and expensive—gold-and-orange iridescent piece to use for the sun in the center. "Nice job, guys," Addie said as she calculated the total.

"It's going to be great," Rosie said. "Just like the mosaic I made for Tess. Dev said I could bring it in and show you."

"I look forward to seeing it." Addie smiled at Rosie's enthusiasm as the young girl lifted Dev's box of supplies and carried it to the work area at the back of the shop, where the others waited.

"Great way to drum up some business." Dev pulled his wallet from a back pocket. "Now comes the hard part."

Addie gave him her strictly business smile. "Working with stained glass is a fun and relaxing hobby."

"Was that the first lesson?"

"No." She stepped from behind her counter and led the way toward her first group of students. "It's a mantra. Tax-free."

The joined the group, and Dev took the spot beside Rosie at one side of the class table. He extended a hand. "Mr. Hawley? Dev Chandler. Calculus."

"I know who you are. And it's Virgil, now that I'm retired and you're old enough to think about settling down."

"What makes you think I'm not already settled down?"

Virgil narrowed his eyes. "This your kid?"

Dev glanced at Rosie. "No."

"Got any of your own?"

"No."

"A wife?"

"No."

"A mortgage?"

Dev hesitated, his smile collapsing at the edges. "No."

Though Addie was secretly enjoying the grilling, she took pity on her best-paying student. "Sorry to interrupt, but we're running a little late. I'd like to get started."

"I'm ready." Virgil pulled his glasses from the bridge of his nose and scrubbed the lenses on the tail of his faded cotton shirt. "Mr. Chandler, as usual, was the tardy one."

"Had to pick up my assistant." Dev nudged Rosie. "Rosie Quinn, this is Virgil Hawley, the meanest math teacher who ever taught at Cove Central High School."

"Did you ever give Dev an F?" Rosie asked.

"Never had the chance." Virgil narrowed his eyes at Dev. "Young fellow always was too smart for his own good."

Rosie slumped on her stool, obviously disappointed. "What about Addie? Did you ever teach her?"

"Yes, I did."

"And now I'm returning the favor," Addie cut in quickly, changing the subject to pattern shears before her own math scores were revealed.

AN HOUR LATER, Dev's neck was stiff with tension. He was having flashbacks to kindergarten traumas. Tracing lines, wielding scissors, handling glue. His old adversaries.

"Not again." Rosie sighed impatiently and set aside the extra set of shears Addie had loaned her. She pried the pattern paper and shears from Dev's cramping fingers and tugged a wrinkled wad of paper from his jammed tool. "Addie told you—you're only supposed to cut a fraction of an inch at a time."

"Want to finish the rest for me?" He shoved his share of the pattern in her direction. Tess hadn't been pleased to hear that Dev had signed up for Addie's class, and she wasn't sure it was the right place for a ten-year-old. But Rosie had insisted, promising to be on her best behavior. And Dev was counting on Rosie to set a good example for him.

"How much will you pay me?" Rosie asked.

"You're paying her to sit through class with you?" Barb sighed her disapproval as she slathered glue on one of her pieces and stuck it to a square of glass. "How much do craft class assistants charge these days?"

"I'm not getting paid for this. Not yet, anyway," Rosie added with a meaningful glance at Dev. "But he's paying me fifty dollars to walk his grandmother's dogs."

Barb frowned. "Fifty dollars is a lot of money for a child."

"I'm not a child." Rosie looked as though she wanted to climb across the table and give Barb's unnaturally red hair a hard yank. "I'm just younger than you. *Lots* younger. At least forty or fifty years younger."

"Rosie." Addie pulled the jar of rubber cement from

Dev's box of supplies. "Let's make sure you glue that sun piece to the right spot on that special orange glass you and Dev picked out."

His pretty teacher cast a sympathetic look his way with those big, beautiful eyes. He'd seen that look before, when he'd discovered he'd turned his carbon paper upside down and traced his entire pattern onto the wrong place. He'd thought this class would give him a chance to spend more time with Addie. He hadn't realized it would also give her a chance to watch him make a fool of himself.

And he couldn't quit, as much as he wanted to. He couldn't even make an escape, not now that so many people had wrapped him up in so many expectations. Rosie was looking forward to coming back to Addie's next three lessons. Tess was counting on him to keep Rosie occupied in the afternoons. Geneva was relying on him to keep watch over Chandler House and feed her dogs. He had Jack and Charlie's wedding to attend and a poker game to host.

And Addie—what did she expect from him?

Today's lust for his teacher was complicated by his guilt over last night's search through his father's papers. He'd found several cancelled checks made out to "Cash"—checks for large amounts, in Lena's hand-writing and cashed by Jonah. Checks that didn't seem to match any business expenses or charitable dona-tions.

Checks that seemed to cast a shadow of suspicion over Lena's innocence. But there was no proof, no answers in the paperwork.

Geneva had claimed that Jonah had made several foolish investments. And Dev had been a fool to think he'd find something that had eluded the accountants and investigators who'd combed through the family's business records searching for a clue to the missing funds.

He'd returned to Carnelian Cove determined to find the answers to his own questions about his father's affairs. Now he wanted those answers more than ever—to give Addie and her mother the closure they deserved.

He looked up to see Addie over Teddi's shoulder, helping her position her pattern pieces on her glass squares. One of the funky clips in Addie's hair shifted to the side, and a perfect blond spiral slipped over her shoulder to brush along her breast.

Dev lowered his gaze to his shears and concentrated on how much he hated cutting out these stupid pattern pieces instead of how much he wanted to pull Addie into his lap, and kiss her senseless. She'd taste of that soda she was sipping, cool and tart and effervescent.

He waited for his breathing to slow to normal and for his heart to stop pounding against his ribs. Then he sighed inwardly and picked up the next pattern piece. One class hour down, fifteen more to go.

ADDIE SPRAWLED ON the petite, blue-checked sofa in Tess's living room on Thursday night, a plump pillow scrunched beneath her head and one leg dangling over the stylishly curved arm. Her second stained-glass class had exhausted her more than the first—probably because Dev's work had been a bigger disaster. She hadn't expected him to be so clumsy with his hands, since he'd been a star athlete in high school. Of course, sprinting down a basketball court on a fast break or smashing a serve across a tennis net required different skills than grinding small pieces of glass that had been awkwardly cut.

She glanced at her watch, expecting Tess's cell phone to ring at any moment. Maudie had dragged Charlie down to the city the day before to buy the wedding dress, and Charlie had promised to report in person when she and her mother returned this evening.

As soon as they got a good look at Charlie's dress, Addie and Tess would choose their own outfits. Addie didn't care what she wore, and since fashion mattered far more to Tess, Addie was willing to leave the shopping up to her. Instead, Addie flipped through the pages of a bridal magazine, scanning the pages for white-flower bouquets. "I still can't get over the fact that Charlie decided to have an all-white wedding," she said.

"At first I thought she was just chickening out on the color selection." Tess handed Addie a glass of iced tea and then sank into a deep chair across the room, careful not to spill her own beverage. "But now I think it's a brilliant idea."

"It sure simplified the wedding shower decorations." Addie straightened, took a sip of tea and then set the glass on a nearby table before collapsing back against the pillows. "Too bad we have to get up at the crack of dawn on Saturday to put them up."

"You're the one with the shop that never closes."

"Closed shop, no sales." Addie yawned and dropped the magazine to the floor. She shifted to her side, snuggling into the downy sofa cushions. "Not that many sales anyway, but at least I know I've tried my darndest."

"How are the classes going?"

"Doesn't Rosie fill you in?"

"Only to tell me what a total loser my cousin is."

"He's not that bad, not really." When Tess gave a disbelieving snort, Addie grinned. "All right," she admitted, "he's *awful*. I never imagined one person could be so bad with every step of the process."

Tess leaned over one arm of her chair to peer around the corner, down the hallway leading to her room, where she'd left Quinn's daughter with a huge bowl of popcorn and a DVD. And then she turned back to face Addie. "My little spy also says he spends most of his time watching you."

Addie picked up the magazine and made a show of studying the cover. "They all do. I'm the teacher. I demonstrate things."

"Things, hmm?" Tess set her glass on the fussy French table beside her chair. "Your face is getting red."

"I hate it when that happens." Addie tossed the magazine back on the floor. "And I'm really too tired for one of your interrogations tonight."

"That's why I didn't bring out the thumbscrews." Tess grabbed one of her bare feet and tucked it beneath her, settling into her quarter-lotus gossip position. "Come on, Addie. Spill."

"There's nothing to report. Nothing has happened. Maybe a couple of interested looks, but—ugh." Addie grabbed the pillow from beneath her head and smashed it against her face for a few mortified seconds. "That sounds so high school," she mumbled against the scratchy wool.

"I didn't catch that last part. And stop molesting that chicken."

Addie pulled the pillow from her face and smoothed a hand over the needlepoint rooster posing on the sham. "I said I feel like I'm back in high school."

"Because we're gossiping about boys on a week-night?" Tess shrugged and reached for her tea. "I'm sitting here waiting for an old friend to show up with her wedding dress. I'm in a sentimental mood."

"Maybe that's all I'm feeling, too. Sentimental." Addie rolled to her back with a sigh. "Remember that awful board game we used to play when we were kids? That one where you could send your opponent back to square one? Just when I think I'm making some progress with my social life, Dev shows up and knocks me out of play."

"I take it you're referring to Mick." Tess shook her head. "Too bad. *Way* too bad. Nice guy."

"*Extremely* nice guy." Addie flung an arm over her eyes. "What's wrong with me? Why can't I appreciate the nice guys I've met and forget about the one who has trouble deciding whether he wants to risk something as simple as a friendship?"

"I might have had something to do with that. And I feel awful about it," Tess added in a rush when Addie stared at her. "I warned Dev to leave you alone."

"You did? Oh." Addie's lips turned up in the beginning of a smile.

"What do you mean, 'oh'?"

"When did you give him this warning?" Addie asked. "Before or after he signed up for my class?"

Tess settled back in her chair with a sigh. "Before. An entire week before."

"Before Geneva's party?"

Tess nodded.

"And yet he sought me out for a talk that day. And he signed himself up for four afternoons at my shop. Not to mention coming in on two other occasions to buy things for Rosie." Addie's smile turned wicked. "Guess you're not as scary as you think."

"I don't know what to think." Tess chewed on the side of her thumb, an old, nervous habit. "I know all this time you're spending with Dev is making you happy. But remember—he's got a lousy track record."

Tess's doorbell chimed.

"It's Charlie!" Rosie raced through the room. "I'll get it."

"Let's drop the talk about Dev." Addie swung her legs off the sofa and stood. "This is Charlie's night."

"I survived," Charlie announced as Rosie dragged her into the room. She draped a large garment bag over the back of Tess's ladder-back chair. "Just barely. Mom wanted to stay another night and shop for shoes and lingerie—lingerie, ugh!—but we've got that big pour out near Fern River tomorrow, and we're short one driver."

"Got to keep your priorities straight." Addie ran a hand down the bag, savoring the anticipation.

Charlie and Rosie both grabbed for the zipper.

"Oh, no you don't." Tess scrambled from her chair to snatch the bag from their prying fingers. "In my room. Put this on and then come out here to show us."

"Yes, please," Addie said, cutting off Charlie's protest before she could make it. "We want to see it on you."

"I'll help." Rosie stood and tugged Charlie by the hand. "Come on."

Addie carried her tea glass into Tess's kitchen and rinsed it in the sink. She was tiring of all the concern and advice, tiring of the entire situation. She wanted to enjoy her friends' wedding plans without suspecting Charlie and Tess felt guilty because they each had something that Addie didn't: a man.

She made her way back to Tess's front room as Rosie peered around the corner. "Are you ready?" Rosie asked.

"Ready," Tess told her. She grabbed Addie's hand and gave it a hard squeeze as Charlie made her entrance. "Omigod. *Omigod*. Charlie—is that you?"

Charlie laughed and spun in a subtle cloud of soft-white satin and chiffon, as delicate and airy as a dandelion puff. "You've seen me in a dress before."

"I've never seen you looking like a bride before." Tess dropped Addie's hand and clasped both of her own beneath her chin. "I love it. I absolutely adore it. Let me see the back again."

While Tess crooned over Charlie's dress, Addie stood apart, enjoying the scene, giddy with excitement. She was incredibly thrilled for her friends and delighted to share in moments like these. There may have been no search for a white dress or plans for cakes and flowers in her immediate future, but that didn't mean she couldn't reach out and seize a big helping of her own happiness.

And she swore to herself, as she hugged her friends, that she would find a way to do precisely that.

CHAPTER ELEVEN

Two POKER GAMES IN as many weeks didn't exactly qualify as a tradition, Dev told himself as he shuffled and dealt the first hand Friday night. But the fact that Bud had just mentioned he'd cleared a Friday night date two weeks from this one sure felt like a dangerous pattern.

"Can't make it." Jack grinned. "Wedding rehearsal. With all the trimmings."

"Bachelor-party poker could work." Rusty chewed his wad of gum for a while and then signaled for another card. "Start later. Play longer. Drink more. Unless you've got other plans."

Jack shook his head. "Sorry to disappoint y'all, but my only plans for that evening include dinner with the honored guests and a quiet drink with my best man."

"Charlie's brother, right?" Dev raised the betting another nickel. "I heard he'd moved to the city."

Jack nodded. "Got into some fancy art school, and Tess fixed him up with a job at her mother's gallery. He's happy as a pig in slop."

Rusty took the pot, and Jack dealt the next hand.

Quinn pulled his chirping cell phone from his jeans pocket and checked the number. "Hey there," he said with a gooey smile that meant Tess was on the other end. "What's up?"

The others scooped up their cards to examine their hands while Quinn listened patiently. "Tess wants to know if there's a ladder in the house," he said after a few seconds.

"At Chandler House?" Dev shrugged. How the hell would he know? "Why does she want a ladder?"

Quinn offered him the phone. "You want to ask her that?"

Dev lifted his hands in self-defense. "Never mind."

"Tell her I'll drop one off in the morning," Jack said, "but it'll have to be early. I want to get to the office by six."

"You can drop it off on the front porch." Dev reached beneath his T-shirt to scrub a hand over his belly. "No way in hell I'm going to be up and around at that time of day."

"Tess says six'll be fine," Quinn said with a grin, "since that's when she and Addie are planning on getting here to decorate."

"She's kidding, right?" Dev shoved away from the table and stalked to the kitchen for another beer.

"Tess says you can carry the ladder in when you meet her to open up the house."

"Hell." Dev lowered the bottle before he could take the first sip. "Why does she have to get started so early?"

Quinn offered him the phone again, and Dev waved it away.

"Women." Rusty slumped in his chair, his jaw working furiously on his gum. "Why can't they figure out a way to have a wedding shower without messing things up for us?"

"Us?" Dev scowled over his bottle. "I don't see you

setting your alarm for the crack of dawn on a Saturday. Sorry," he quickly added when the three construction workers stared at him.

"Guess I'll be the only one sleeping in tomorrow." Bud spread his cards on the table and scooped the chips toward his pile. "Winner all around."

"Except you've got a wife telling you what to do with your weekend," Rusty pointed out.

"You've got Quinn telling you what to do with most of yours," Bud shot back.

"I don't mind waking up to the alarm to find a beautiful woman beside me," Jack said. "Bet Quinn here feels the same."

Quinn slipped the phone back into his pocket. "Haven't had enough of those experiences with the beautiful woman in my life to know for sure. Want to take Rosie for the night so I can test your theory?"

"Kids." Rusty leaned his bony elbows on the table. "They sure can mess things up for a guy."

"They're okay." Dev strolled back to the table and took his seat. "Rosie's definitely in the okay category."

"You volunteering for an overnight, Uncle Dev?" asked Quinn.

"I might consider it, later in the summer." He thought it might be fun to rent some DVDs, pop some corn. Tess would owe him, big-time—that was worth one evening with Rosie.

Quinn's phone chirped again. Rusty threw down his cards with a curse. "Bet the guys who play in the big game across town don't put up with this crap."

The movement around the table stilled, and Bud glared at Rusty. Quinn glanced at them both with a frown, stood and walked from the room, his phone to his ear.

"What big game?" Jack asked.

"High stakes." Rusty shrugged—a jerky, dismissive movement—and picked up his cards to study them as if they held the answers to all life's questions. "Don't know much else."

"Poker?" Dev asked. He waited for Bud to meet his gaze. "Here in the Cove?"

"A rumor. That's all it is. If there had been a game like that, it ended a long time ago." Bud threw down his cards and headed toward the kitchen. "Anyone else want a beer?"

Dev won most of the pots that evening, his luck as good as ever. Luck had always been on his side, it seemed. Unlike his father, who had been unlucky in love and unlucky with his business investments.

Maybe his father had been unlucky at play, too. Maybe there was another explanation for the curious holes in the Chandler profits, for the sizable checks Addie's mother had written out to "Cash" and handed over to Jonah. For the missing sum of sixty-two thousand dollars that had nearly landed her in jail for embezzlement.

Gambling debts.

THE SHANTYMAN HADN'T CHANGED much over the years. Dev recognized the bass beat of an old tune thumping from the same domed jukebox in the corner. The same black-framed photos on the dark plank walls, the old billiard table angled across one corner, the familiar tacky feel of the floor beneath his feet. Looked like the typical Sunday-night patrons at the bar—a couple of off-season fishermen hunched over their brews and staring glassy-eyed at a closed-captioned baseball game rerun.

Johnnie Murphy was still tending bar here, too. He

leaned on the counter, close enough to his customers to catch an order but far enough away to avoid any conversation that might start up between innings. Johnnie wasn't into idle chat. Why he'd chosen employment in a pub was one of life's mysteries.

"Hey, Dev." Johnnie nodded as Dev took a stool down at his end, far from the sports fans. "Heard you were back."

"Yeah." Dev gave his order and watched Johnnie pour a finger of whiskey into a thick glass. "Pretty quiet around here."

"Summer's always slow. Students on vacation, locals at their summer cabins."

"Never could figure out the appeal of a summer cabin." Dev spun his glass on the counter. "Makes you feel obligated to take the same vacation, over and over. You got one?" he asked.

"A cabin? Would I be here if I did?" Johnnie trudged off to check on his other customers. It was a tough choice between tolerating aimless sports chatter and having to make small talk, but in the end the bartender drifted back Dev's way.

"Got a friendly poker game going up at my place the past couple of weeks," Dev said. "Nickel bets," he added when Johnnie didn't respond. "Nothing to give the women back home anything to worry about."

Johnnie gave him a bland stare.

Dev sipped his drink. "One of the guys said he'd heard a rumor about some high-stakes card games around the Cove."

Johnnie lowered his gaze and rubbed at an invisible spot with his clean white cloth. "Might have heard the same rumor."

Dev took another sip and waited.

"Couple of big-shot lumbermen had a regular game going in a suite at the Cove Redwood Inn." Johnnie's gaze flicked up to meet Dev's for a second. "But that was a few years back."

"Back when my dad was still alive?"

"Yeah. Back then."

At least nine years ago. "Nothing since?"

Johnnie flipped the cloth over his shoulder, placed his palms against the edge of the counter and leaned toward Dev. The bartender's expression was less welcoming than usual. "You thinking I might know how to hook you up with something like that?"

"No."

"Good." Johnnie stalked off to watch the silent game on the screen above the bar.

Dev wasn't all that sure the bartender would return to this end of the counter any time soon. He sat and stared at the bottles clogging the shelves around the mirror. Probably the same bottles that had been there for years, too.

He shoved his drink aside and let his mind wander through the memories this place had jogged loose. Challenging Bud to a game of pool to see which one of them was going to run a stolen crab pot up Mrs. Stelzer's flagpole. Dancing oh-so-slow on this sticky floor, his hand spread over Shelley Terzian's soft butt while he tried to figure out the logistics of sex in a sports car.

The tune in the jukebox changed to one he'd heard the night he'd watched geeky Alan Schwartz lead Addie onto the floor of the high school gym for her first homecoming dance. She'd been so pretty that night, all dolled up in her strapless pink dress, her long hair pinned up in the kind of tangle that made a guy want to release it. Dev's date had fumed on the sidelines and then stomped off to the ladies' room when he'd leaned against the wall to watch the dance instead of taking to the floor, too.

He should tell Addie about his research, tell her what he'd discovered so far about her mother and his father. He was beginning to feel guilty about keeping this from her, worried how she'd react if she found out what he'd been up to.

Tomorrow. He'd tell her tomorrow. If he got a chance. And the timing was right. If she—

Coward.

He glanced at Johnnie, who was still pretending an interest in the game. Eventually the bartender would be forced to head back Dev's way, if only to kick him out the door at closing time.

Dev took one last sip, barely wetting his lips. He hadn't come in to drink, and he didn't want the rest of the whiskey. He'd wanted to find out whether his father had enjoyed the occasional poker game, too. Johnnie might not have answered all of his questions or revealed the names of the men involved, but he'd confirmed Rusty's rumor.

And there were only two big-shot lumbermen who'd been friends of Jonah Chandler.

FIVE MINUTES AFTER Addie had slipped into her apartment on Monday to nuke some leftover pizza for a late-afternoon snack, the bell rang above her door. She dashed back into her shop to find Dev standing near the entry and holding two cones from the ice-cream parlor down the street.

He nodded at one of the cones. "Double fudge ripple."

He'd remembered her favorite. Ridiculously pleased, she crossed the shop, but he lifted the cone out of reach before she could take it.

"Not so fast," he said. "These are outside cones. The ice cream loses its flavor indoors."

"I have to work."

"That's all you ever do. Work, work, work."

"Bills, bills, bills," she answered.

"I'll make it up to you." He took a slow, sensual taste of the other cone, the expression in his eyes hot enough to melt the ice cream.

She swallowed. "How will you do that?"

"I'm working on it. I can be productive, too."

He stepped outside, and since he'd taken her double fudge ripple with him, she had no choice but to follow. She flipped her sign to Closed, locked her door and collected her cone.

He took her hand and led her on a casual stroll down Cove Street, as if they were two tourists window-shopping their way toward the waterfront. "When was the last time you left your shop?" he asked.

"On Saturday. For Charlie's wedding shower." She licked her ice cream and enjoyed the sensations of coolness inching down her throat and sunshine warming her skin. And his strong fingers laced through hers. Gulls glided overhead, screaming abuse at a fisherman dumping his bait in the bay.

It should be a simple, natural thing to hold a man's hand on a walk like this, but this was Dev's hand. There had never been anything simple about being with Dev, and nothing natural about their relationship.

"Not yesterday?" he asked.

"There wasn't any need. I've got food in the fridge and plenty of work to keep me busy."

"It was beautiful yesterday."

"It's beautiful today." She squeezed his hand, delighted with the mild weather and the unexpected treat, with the considerate company and the blissful contentment. "Thank you for reminding me to notice."

"You've got to get out more."

"I'm out now."

"So you are." He grinned at her, and then his step slowed and his smile faded. He seemed to have something on his mind, as though he were about to say—or do—something important. Something very serious. She slowed, too, wondering what would come next.

He stopped and faced her as she bit into a ribbon of gooey fudge, and he stared at her mouth as she licked a bit of ice cream from her lip.

Would he kiss her today? Was that why he'd come? Would he taste of butter pecan and salted air? Would he whisper her name again and make her melt against him?

"Addie," he said as he leaned closer.

"Yes?"

He hesistated. Straightened.

"How are the windows coming?"

Geneva's windows. He'd come to check on her progress, not to kiss her. "Fine."

"Not keeping you from enjoying life and getting out once in a while, I hope."

"No." She tossed the remains of the cone to the complaining gulls. "But I'd better get back."

"I made a solid start on my story today." He told her

about the characters, gesturing with his cone and with their joined hands as they started back toward her shop. She waited for him to release his grip on her, but he never did. He'd never touched her for so long before today.

She should be grateful for that, she told herself. It was a start. What that start was, she had no idea. Nothing simple, that was for sure.

Dev stopped on the corner one block from her shop. "Is that Lena?"

Addie watched her mother get out of her car and head toward A Slice of Light. Childish panic tugged her hand from Dev's. "Yes."

"Looks like she's waiting for you." He slipped his hands into his pockets. "Go ahead."

"Dev, I—"

"It's all right. " He backed toward the curb. "Thanks for the walk."

"Thanks for the ice cream."

She stood in place until he'd ducked around Mona's coffeeshop, and then she hurried up the street. "Mom. What a nice surprise."

"Sorry to bother you right after closing," Lena said as Addie unlocked the door. Her mother held a plastic-wrapped plate of brownies in her hand. "I've been running late all day today."

"I'll forgive you if those are what I think they are."

"My frosted double-fudge brownies." Lena handed Addie the plate and followed her back to the apartment. "Even after cutting the recipe in half, there are still too many for me to eat. But every once in a while I get a craving for them."

Addie grinned. "Lucky for me you end up having to share."

"Is this your dinner?" Lena pointed to Addie's pizza with a disapproving look. "You need some vegetables or fruit. I hope you're taking your vitamins. With the schedule you keep—"

"Hey, I learned from a pro how to take care of myself." Addie set the brownies on her compact kitchen counter and poured a glass of the cold brewed tea she kept in her refrigerator. She handed the glass to her mother. "I'd offer you some brownies, but I'll bet you've already had your quota today."

"Yes." Lena took the glass and pressed a hand to her trim waist. "More than I should have. Please, don't let me keep you." She waved toward Addie's cooling dinner.

"That's okay. I can reheat it again." Addie collected her own glass of tea and joined her mother at the little table in the center of her open apartment space. "By the way, Charlie loved the shower gift you sent."

"I'm so glad. She's a sweet girl."

"I wish you had come to the party and watched her open it."

Lena's smile disappeared. "You know I'll have nothing to do with the Chandlers."

"Maybe Charlie's wedding is a good reason to put all that behind you."

Addie's mother slowly spun her glass on the table. "Jonah Chandler ruined my life. He set me up with those checks he made me write, and then he framed me for theft. And Geneva—" Lena paused, her features pinched with strain. "Geneva refused to admit what her son had done."

Addie had heard this refrain a dozen times. Her mother seemed to believe that if she told her version of the story often enough, it would eventually become the truth.

Delusions about the past seemed to be something the Sutton women had in common.

Seized by a sudden urge to change the pattern, Addie braced herself for her mother's reaction. "Dev Chandler is one of the students in my stained-glass class," she said quickly, as if the announcement were a bandage she was ripping off a fresh wound.

Lena's mouth firmed in an angry, stubborn line. "I don't suppose you could have told him you didn't have room for him in class?"

"Why would I do that? His tuition money is as good as anyone else's."

"Just like Geneva's money was good for those repairs. I don't like this." Lena rose and walked an aimless path through the apartment. "Dev has always had his eye on you—for no good reason, I'm sure."

"Maybe he found me interesting," Addie said, ignoring the prick at her pride, "or attractive. Maybe he wanted to be my friend."

"He was a troublemaker. I'm sure he still is."

"He's a very nice man who is watching his grandmother's house and pets while she's gone. And spending his afternoons taking care of Quinn's little girl."

"Why are you defending him?"

"Because he deserves it. He's done nothing wrong," Addie said. "He's Dev Chandler, not Jonah."

Her mother's obvious shock at Addie's argument was quickly displaced by guilt-inducing pain, her eyes welling with tears. "Obviously I can no longer advise you to stay away from him," Lena said. "You're a grown woman who's entitled to make her own mistakes. I just hope you know what you're doing."

She headed toward Addie's door.

"Thank you for the brownies," Addie called after her.

"You're welcome," her mother answered in a strained voice. She closed the shop door behind her with a quiet click.

Addie rose from her chair, slowly and stiffly, as if she'd aged fifty years since she'd taken her seat. She dumped her dirty dishes in her sink and ran water over them. Her appetite—even for homemade double-fudge brownies with buttercream frosting—had vanished.

CHAPTER TWELVE

DEV FOLLOWED A SHAPELY receptionist down a long, darkly paneled hall on the second floor of the Coast Redwood Products building on Tuesday morning. It was rare to find redwood used so extravagantly, and seeing it crafted in old-fashioned, vertical grooves like this always made him aware of Carnelian Cove's unique place in the lumber industry.

"Devlin." Harve Billings stood as Dev entered his office. He walked around his massive desk, hand extended. "Good to see you again."

"Thank you for agreeing to meet with me, Harve." Dev shook his hand, noticing the white edging the gray in the old lumberman's hair and the sagging skin below his watery blue eyes. He must have been nearing seventy by now, and he looked it. "I appreciate it," Dev added.

Harve waved him toward one of the high-backed leather chairs arranged around a low table in one corner of his office and nodded at the receptionist as she closed the door, shutting them in. "How's Geneva?" he asked as he settled into a matching chair. "I haven't seen her since the wine auction. When was that? May? Yes, May, I think."

"She's fine. She's in the Caribbean, on a cruise."

Harve's chest rose and fell in a series of spasms that passed for a chuckle. "Good for her. She's got more energy than any two people I know."

"Yes, sir."

"You're not going to 'sir' me through the rest of this visit, are you?"

"No."

"Good. Makes me feel older than I already am." Harve cleared his throat. "And you? What are you up to these days? Still teaching in San Francisco?"

"I had a couple of classes last term. I thought I'd take a break. Do some writing."

"Good, good." Harve nodded his approval. "Well then," he said, lacing his fingers across his belly, "what brings you down here?"

Dev paused. He still hadn't thought of a subtle way to introduce the topic he wanted to discuss, and Harve hadn't given him any openings. He was left with no alternative but to simply say it straight out. "Since I've been back, a couple of old friends and I have started up a friendly little card game."

Harve nodded. His expression didn't change. Dev wondered if he was seeing Harve's poker face.

"Nothing high stakes," Dev continued. "Nickel and dime antes. Just a social game."

Harve nodded again. "Sometimes those are the best kind."

"They can be. We're enjoying it." Dev lifted an ankle over one knee, settling back. "Sometimes, I imagine, it's equally enjoyable to play for higher stakes."

Harve's nodding continued. He didn't say a word.

"Someone told me there used to be some high-stakes poker here in the Cove," Dev said. "Years ago."

Harve's nodding stopped, but his expression remained neutral. "I suppose that's a possibility."

"Did you ever hear of any games like that?"

"Can't say I did."

Cleverly phrased…and a dead end. "I was wondering if my father ever played."

"You could ask Geneva," Harve pointed out.

"I don't remember them discussing it." Dev smiled. "Poker games—friendly or otherwise—aren't usually something a man discusses with his mother."

"Or his grandmother."

Dev smiled and waited. Harve rubbed his thumbs together and smiled back.

The phone on Harve's desk buzzed. "Excuse me," he said as he walked across his office to get it.

Dev stood and took a closer look at the old photos hanging on Harve's office walls. Men in mustaches and suspenders and boots, posed around a giant redwood stump. Immense logs stacked behind a black iron steam donkey. A view of Carnelian Cove as it looked one hundred years earlier, showing the commercial buildings along the bay and the gridlike streets of the older neighborhoods nearby.

"That's my granddaddy." Harve rejoined Dev and pointed a thick finger at a different photo, one of a wiry man standing beside a team of oxen. "He worked in a camp out past the bluff."

"I wonder if he knew my great-grandfather."

Harve continued to stare at the photo. After a few seconds, he let out a long sigh. "Your father was a good friend."

"I appreciate that."

"He had his faults, I suppose, but he meant well. He

always meant well." Harve's features grew stern. "He had high hopes for you."

"I wish I'd known him better."

"He died too young, that's for sure."

Harve paced to the window. He shoved his suit jacket back as he slid his hands into his pockets and stared out over the bay. "I'm sure the local authorities would take a dim view of the kind of high-stakes game you're talking about."

"I'm not interested in playing. I know it's illegal."

"Good." Harve glanced over his shoulder and gave Dev one decisive nod. "Keep that in mind."

"It was illegal back then, too."

"That's right."

"Did my father play?" Dev asked.

Harve's shoulders rose and fell on another long sigh. "Yes."

"The night he died?"

Harve shook his head. "I don't know anything about that night."

There was more Dev wanted to know, but Harve's features revealed his regret. The lumberman wouldn't be providing any more information.

Not today, anyway.

THAT AFTERNOON, as Dev glued the same damn piece of disintegrating pattern paper to the same damn piece of wavy blue glass—for the third time—he no longer suspected he'd never make another stained-glass picture. He was certain of it.

He'd never thought of himself as a quitter. He'd stuck it out until the end of the season with his first soccer team, even after he'd broken a wrist in a fall and decided playing ball with one's feet was a game for idiots. He'd stuck it out in choir for a semester, even after his teacher had discovered he couldn't carry a tune and had begged him to lip-sync at the class concert.

But the thought of spending another afternoon like this in Addie's shop made him consider poisoning himself so he could call in sick on Thursday.

His glass cutting during the second class had been so badly done that he'd needed extra time at the grinder. While the others in the class had quickly smoothed the sharp edges, Dev had spent hours trimming extra glass and regluing sopped pattern pieces.

Addie leaned in close to his side, her daisies-and-lemonade scent making his vision blur and his mouth go dry. "How's it going?" she asked.

"Fine. Nearly ready to give it another shot." He waited for her to step away—to give him space to breathe again—and then he shoved back his stool. It scraped across her floor with a jarring squawk, and the noise made him wince.

Shake it off, Chandler, he ordered himself as he stalked to the grinder. He slipped his safety glasses over his face, flipped on the machine, and slowly passed the glass against the bit, determined to get the straight edge straightened out. A few seconds later, one side of the pattern paper curled up. With a muttered curse, he peeled the rest away, dabbed the paper and glass with a shop towel and headed back to his seat.

"Not a word," he warned Rosie as he handed her the damp paper and glass. "Not one."

She heaved a dramatic sigh as she spread the pieces

beside two other sets of disasters, and then she returned to her task of gently scrubbing old glue from the dried patterns.

He picked up one of the papers and began to reapply the glue, adding plenty to make sure it stayed stuck this time. A thick glob of rubber cement oozed from beneath the paper as he pressed it to the glass, and when he pulled his fingers away, the paper came with them, glued to his hand. "Damn," he muttered.

"Are you still working on that same piece?" Rosie peeled the gooey mess from his fingers. "Jeez, you're slow."

The knot between Dev's shoulder blades tightened.

"The girl's right." Virgil lifted one of his own glass pieces, examined the edge against the overhead light and nodded with satisfaction. "Never saw anyone so inept at such simple tasks in my entire life."

Shut up, Dev silently ordered Virgil.

"I think he's doing fine." Barb gave Dev one of her saccharine smiles. "Work that involves small motor skills is sometimes more difficult for men."

Shut up.

"Is that one of those sexist comments?" Rosie stared at Barb with poorly feigned innocence. "Is it? One of my teachers told my class about politically incorrect speech last year, and I'm trying to figure out if I understand what it all means."

Addie pulled a cell phone from her apron pocket and handed it to Rosie. "Why don't you give Tess a call and see when she's coming to pick you up?"

"Not so fast." Dev plucked the phone from the girl's hand and passed it back to Addie. "If she doesn't stay and help me finish this, I'll be here all night."

I'll be here all night. Addie froze, her fingers covered his on the phone, and he treated himself to the fantasy that she could feel the heat rushing through him. And then she took the phone from him, rubbed away the rubber cement residue and slipped it back into her pocket before moving to the other side of the table to check Virgil's work.

"All right." Rosie gave Dev a high five and then handed him the next piece to glue. "You're probably going to need me to help you on Thursday, too. Virgil's right. You suck."

Dev was beginning to see why Tess got along so well with her soon-to-be stepdaughter. They were a lot alike. "If I bring you back on Thursday—and the chances of that are growing slimmer by the minute—you won't be able to help with the soldering."

"That's okay." Rosie shrugged. "I want to be here to see you mess up that part, too."

Dev grabbed the glue wand and smoothed the goo over the paper. And then he stopped and stared with horror at the tiny, shredded triangle of paper stuck to the edge of the brush: the ruined corner of his pattern paper. "Damn."

"Now what?" Rosie peeked over his shoulder. "You ripped it? Oh, man. You're toast."

"Let me see, Dev." Addie took the sticky paper bits and lined them up on her palm.

He cleared his throat. "Can you fix it?"

She gave him a kindly smile, the kind of pitying, patient look any instructor would bestow on the imbecile in her class. "No. Rosie's right. You're toast."

It took him a second to figure out she was teasing. A thrilling second in which he dreamed of a dishon-

orable discharge. An escape from craft prison. He'd
rise from his wobbly metal stool and walk out that
shop door, a free man.

And in the next second, Addie's apologetic smile
turned deliciously wicked, deepening her dimples. A
familiar, gut-deep tug pulled him under, and he wanted
to do whatever it took to stick this out. Even if that
meant grinding every bit of glass in her shop to shapeless nubs.

"We're going to try something different." She
reglued the pattern piece to his blue glass, pulled a red
glass-marking pen from his supply box and filled in the
missing corner.

As she worked, the soft pink cotton of her T-shirt
lifted and fell as she breathed—up and down, in and
out—and the taunting shadow of cleavage above its
V-shaped neckline shifted like a curl of smoke. Warm,
moist puffs of air brushed Dev's face. One perfect
tendril of spun-gold hair slipped from behind her ear
to lay against her collarbone, the turned-up ends beck-
oning.

She handed him the glass and pointed to the neat
mark on the end. "Now the trick is to grind away the
red. Nothing more," she told him in her teacher's voice.
"You can always remove more glass if you need to. It's
pretty hard to add the missing glass back."

He cleared his throat. "Yeah. I've got it. Thanks."

She moved away, and he stared sightlessly at the
things in his hands, waiting for the pounding, swishing
tidal wave in his chest to subside.

"Earth to Dev," Rosie whispered.

"Hmm?"

"Are you just going to sit there for the rest of the day?"

"No." Dev's hands came into focus, as big and clumsy as ever and still holding the damn glass and glue.

Everything came into focus.

"I'm going to finish this," he said.

CHAPTER THIRTEEN

TESS COLLECTED ROSIE shortly after four for a dentist appointment, and Dev doubled his efforts to catch up with Addie's other students. But as the rest of the class stretched lengths of lead—lining up those molecules—and nipped neat bits of the stuff to begin assembling their pictures on their layout boards, he fell further behind.

Dev tried, again, to slip the orange piece into place. It didn't fit. In fact, it knocked the entire top half out of whack.

Damn.

"I think I'm going to call it a day." Virgil stood with a grunt and stretched. "I have to run a couple of errands before I head home."

Addie suggested he hammer another nail in place to hold one section of his picture more securely and then gave his shoulder a friendly pat. "You've got quite a knack for this," she said.

"I think so, too. I certainly do enjoy it." He pulled on his jacket and lifted a hand in farewell. "See you all again in a couple of days."

Addie strolled to the door with her star pupil, chatting about Thursday's class plans. Dev picked up the orange half circle and trudged back to the grinder bench. He flipped the switch on one of the machines, holding his jaw rigid at the nagging whine as he ran the protruding edge against the bit. Again.

When he returned to the worktable, he found Teddi admiring her work, "Isn't this fun?" she asked. "I've been waiting to see how this is going to look when it's finished."

"Let me see." Barb stood and peered across the table. "Oh, that's beautiful. How's yours coming, Dev?"

"It's getting there." He rolled his shoulders, trying to ease the kink in his neck.

For the hundredth time, he lifted a curving piece to check his work against the light, but he could still see a sliver of green over the edge of the paper. While Barb and Teddi packed their supplies and headed out the door, he stalked back to the grinder to remove another miniscule slice of green. The soaked pattern piece slipped from the glass. Again. "Damn," he muttered.

"Need some help, Dev?" Addie asked.

"No." *I can make a complete mess of this all on my own.* "Thanks."

He blotted the excess water from his work, feeling marginally better when he saw that the green had disappeared for good. And then he turned and saw Addie frowning at his project.

Uh-oh.

He braced for bad news and made his way back to his seat. "What is it?"

She poked at the pale blue glass near the top of his design. "See how this little bump on the orange piece is making these others shift to the right? I think if you trim off just a bit here…" She grabbed his red pen and marked a tiny arc. "Just along this spot. Remember, don't take off too much—"

"Because I can always take off more the next time," he said, forcing himself to smile.

Great. Another problem piece. And only eleven more of them to finish. He headed back to the grinder.

He wished he hadn't let Rosie choose this pattern. He wished he hadn't noticed that flyer advertising this class. He wished he hadn't returned to Carnelian Cove.

But then he wouldn't be standing here in Addie's shop. He wouldn't have been here to watch her interact with her customers, and he wouldn't have taken a closer look at her art.

He wouldn't have reconnected with one of the best pieces of his past.

He heard Addie's soft, tuneless humming, he glanced over his shoulder to find her sweeping the work area. Outside, early evening lengthened the shadows along Cove Street. Two young mothers pushed strollers past the window, laughing at a shared comment. A yellow balloon tethered to a stroller handle bobbed in the breeze, and a swooping gull dodged out of its way.

Good to know someone was enjoying a nice summer evening.

He dragged his stool closer to the table and dropped onto the seat. "Sorry it's taking me so long. I don't have to stay."

"Take as long as you need to. Art doesn't happen according to schedule." She cast a shy glance in his direction as she wiped the counter near her work sink. "When you're writing, do you take exactly the same amount of time to finish each page?"

"Good point."

"I'll be back in a minute." She opened the elaborately leaded glass door at the rear of the shop and stepped into her apartment, closing the door behind her. A few seconds later an overhead fixture switched on, casting a weak band of light over her indistinct form as she moved toward the rear wall and disappeared from view.

Through the lace curtains, Dev thought he could make out a table and chairs. And was that a cabinet hanging from one of the side walls? A sofa against another?

He wondered if she grew bored with her small world, if she tired of living a few steps from the place where she worked all day. There were shops crowding both sides of hers; her only other view must be of the alley in the rear. There was no assistant to cover for her coffee breaks, no coworker to chat with during the slow times.

The light inside her apartment switched off, and he redirected his gaze to his work as she returned to her shop. He carefully pushed the orange half circle into place, pleased to see it line up neatly with the pieces around it. Next he tried shifting the bottom half of the pattern into place. Still no good.

His stomach rumbled, and he realized he'd never had a chance to grab that quick lunch he'd planned after the meeting with Harve. He'd soon be running on empty—yet more trouble. "Addie?"

She moved to stand beside him. "Let's see what's going on here."

A bandage flexed beneath one of her knuckles as she slowly, carefully pressed and prodded the glass into position. The pale, fading nicks of healing cuts and the random scars of old burns formed a tiny network of jarring contrasts against such delicate, fragile skin. He silently promised them both he'd kiss every one of those marks and make them better.

"Here's the problem," she said. "It's this green piece. See how everything seems to catch on this one corner?"

"Why can't I see that for myself?"

"Practice." She straightened, set her hands at her waist and arched back a little, stretching her spine. Stretching her T-shirt across her breasts. Testing the restraint of a starving, desperate man. "Believe me," she said, "I've spent many long hours maneuvering hundreds of pieces into place in big, complicated patterns."

"I don't want to think about it." He didn't want to think about her breasts, either. He picked up the offending slice of glass and trudged back to the grinder.

"Do you mind if I turn on some music?" she asked.

"As long as it isn't Kabuki."

"Kabuki?"

"Japanese opera," Dev told her. "Sounds like cats being tortured."

"Good thing I'm fresh out of Kabuki CDs."

A few seconds later a jazz trio's smooth improvisation floated over the whir of the grinder. He smiled at her choice, and a layer of tension eased from his neck. "Nice."

"You've been there, haven't you? Japan, I mean." She passed a feather duster over a stack of boxes on one of her shelves. "What's it like?"

"Japanese." He turned to see her outlined in one of her big front windows, the softening light of a beginning sunset touching her hair with gold. "You'd stick out like a sore thumb."

She frowned and moved to the end of the shelving, turning her back on him.

"It's not like what you see on TV," he continued as he headed back to the table. "It's not all cherry trees and geishas. Most of the cities are crowded and not all that attractive at street level. But the other parts—those perfectly sculptured parts you see on postcards—they're amazing. It's like moving through a fantasy."

"I'd like to see it someday. I'd like to travel."

"Then do it."

"You make it sound so easy."

"Easier than getting this thing to work," he muttered as he took his seat.

"You'll figure it out." Setting her duster on her desk, she returned to his side. She grabbed a nearby stool, pulled it close and rested her elbow on the table, her face a few inches from his. "You did such a good job with your other pieces. You're closer than you think."

Her simple praise gave him a crazy thrill, along with a reason to hope he'd make it out of there before midnight. He picked up his ruler. Working from the corners, he pressed the pattern pieces toward the center, toward the orange sun at the heart of the design. The bits of glass seemed to shift and slide against each other as though they were living organisms, and then suddenly everything locked together, holding tight, no gaps in sight. The pattern fell into place with a silent click.

"That's it," she said. "You did it. See how perfectly everything fits together?"

He turned his face toward hers and found the old Addie in her eyes, the old smile on her lips.

Click. Everything fell into place.

"We did it," he said. "We made it work."

"You made it work." Her grin was wide and happy and uncomplicated. "All you had to do was smooth out the bumpy parts."

"You make it sound so easy."

"Like going to Japan?"

"No." He took the opportunity to study, up close, her beautiful features. The cloud-soft curls teasing her forehead, the surprising silver streaks in her dark-blue eyes, the adorable slope of her nose, the lush curves of her cheeks. The slightly stubborn chin, the inviting lips. "As if it were easy to find the one thing I was looking for all this time."

Her smile faded, and she dropped her gaze to the table. She straightened and waved awkwardly in the direction of his project. "Sometimes the answer is right there, in front of you."

"You're right." He caught her wrist as he rose from the stool. "Sometimes it is. All you have to do is look."

She stared at his fingers encircling her arm. "Dev, I—"

"I've been looking for a long, long time."

"You haven't been here that long." She shook her head, and one of the clips in her hair slipped another fraction of an inch to the side. "A few hours is all. It only seems longer be—"

She stiffened with a funny, breathy squeak as he slid a hand along her waist. Her narrow, supple, feminine waist. Slowly, he spread his fingers over her lower back, dipping into the slight indentation along her spine and tracing the subtle bumps below. He wanted to savor every touch, every scent, every sigh, every blush, every flutter. He'd missed so much.

"Because you had to make so many trips to the grinder," she finished in a raspy whisper.

"No, I've been looking for years. And look what I've found." He released her wrist to raise his hand to her hair. He'd been wanting—waiting, for a lifetime—to pull those clips and bands from the top of her head, to watch the sunshine-bright streamers fall around her shoulders, to plunge his hands into the thick, luscious mass and grab fistfuls. And now she was here, standing before him with her eyes wide and locked on his, and her lips parted in a breathless surprise that matched his own.

He released one clip, and another, and dropped them to the floor as his fantasy came to life. And then he slid his fingers through the hair above her ear. Cool, springy silk over heated, inviting skin.

He lowered his gaze from her curls to her face. Yes, look what he'd found—*Addie*. "Addie."

"Yes?"

He lightly pressed his palm against her back, guiding her closer. "Have you been looking?"

"Yes," she whispered. She lifted her hands between them, hesitated, and then settled them over his chest.

"For years?" he asked.

Her throat moved as she swallowed. "Yes."

"Do you think you can smooth out my bumpy parts?"

Her fingers curled, catching the fabric of his T-shirt in tiny folds. "I don't know."

"I wish you'd give it a try." He cupped the back of

her head and shifted still closer. "Will you? Will you try?"

"I—" Her lids fluttered closed as his thigh brushed hers. "I don't know what you want from me."

"Yes, you do." He leaned in and tortured himself with a whiff of her scent. Lemony soap, artist's solvents, faint florals, warm woman. *Addie.* "We could start with a kiss and go from there."

"A kiss?"

"Do you need a demonstration?"

She huffed out a shaky little breath and opened her eyes, tilting back her head to give him a sassy smirk. "I know what a kiss is."

"Yes, but you've never been kissed by me."

Her palms flattened against the muscles of his chest, her fingers sliding over his shirt in a maddening exploration. A frown puckered her brow. "A kiss will change everything. If we do this, we'll never be able to go back to the way things were."

He lowered his head toward hers, tempting her. "Do you mean we'll never be friends again?"

"We're not friends. Not really." Her breath caught in another tiny gasp as his mouth came within a few inches of hers. "You said you weren't sure we could ever be friends."

"I'm a fool." He stroked his hand up her back, gently caging her. "You shouldn't listen to a word I say."

She swayed toward him and paused, tantalizingly close. "Friends don't do what we're thinking of doing."

"No, they don't." He smiled and swept his gaze over her face. "But if we've never been friends, then we don't have anything to lose, do we?"

"I don't want to lose *you*."

"Then hold on tight."

He narrowed the gap between them and waited at the brink, feeling her surrender, inch by inch. A tremor, a sigh, the softening of her spine as she eased into his embrace. The whisper of skin sliding along cotton as she smoothed her hands up his body to circle his neck, the citrusy tang of the cleanser near her work sink, the faint laughter of passersby on Cove Street, the smooth concrete beneath their feet—everything surrounding them seemed to fade into the gathering dusk. The only things he knew were the thudding pressure in his chest, and the moist heat of her breath against his lips. And the need to press his mouth—his body—to hers.

Easy, he reminded himself as he brushed his lips along her jaw. Take it slow. This is Addie. Don't ruin this any more than you already have. Don't take too much at first—you can always take more the next time.

He moved his mouth toward hers, a whisper of a kiss tracing one of her dimples, a subtle move in their slow-motion dance. She retreated the merest fraction of an inch, a hesitant side step. He stilled; she parted her lips. He narrowed the slender gap between them, waiting, willing her to meet him halfway.

And then her lashes drifted down, down over her wonderful blue eyes, and her soft curves touched his body. He wrapped his arms around her, drawing her against him, at last. Their lips met once, twice in a teasing trial—so good, so right. And then they seemed to flow into each other and to fit together with their own silent click.

CHAPTER FOURTEEN

THIS WAS CRAZY, Addie thought as Dev brushed gentle, downy kisses across her cheek and then settled his mouth over hers. This was Dev.

This was Dev's hand fisting her shirt in the back and tugging the hem above her waist. This was Dev's knee shoving between her legs. This was Dev's low groan echoing through her darkening shop. And the thrill of it was more than she could trap and hold inside.

More than she could bear, she realized as she plastered herself against him and tangled her fingers in his hair. More than she could handle, she thought as his arms tightened around her and something clattered to the floor beside them. And then she stopped thinking, and he stopped holding back, and they both started taking in long-starved, greedy gulps.

Addie grasped the collar of Dev's shirt, afraid to let go. *Dev, Dev, oh, Dev.* The words—the thought of him touching her like this, at last—pulsed through her, a chant as rhythmic and natural as her heartbeat. And the feel of him heated every part of her body that came into contact with his—fingertips, arms, breasts, thighs, lips.

His arms banded around her waist to crush her against him, and his hot breath scorched a path over her forehead. She thought he'd whispered something in her ear before he nipped its edge, but she couldn't hear anything above the surflike roar of her blood and that pounding chant.

Dev, Dev.

She shouldn't have thrown herself at him that way, opening to the hot, moist sweep of his tongue through her mouth and answering with a deep, thorough taste of her own. Shouldn't have given him such easy access, letting her head fall back with a groan as he nibbled his way down her throat. Shouldn't have invited more, bending her knee to slide her leg along his until he grasped her thigh, pulled her higher and ground his hips against hers.

But this was Dev, and he was the only man she'd ever really wanted. And this might be her only chance to touch him like this, to test her fantasy of what they could be like together. Oh, she wanted so desperately for it to be *good*. And oh, he made it good, so good, for her.

Dev, Dev.

"Addie. *Addie.*" He tugged at her hair, drawing her head back, bringing their faces close. "I never knew."

"That's because you never—"

Just in time, sanity slipped into the cool sliver of space he'd opened between them, stopping her before she confessed to years of painful, pitiful, unrequited infatuation. "What do you mean, you never knew?" she asked.

"How good this could be." He pressed his mouth to her chin again, teasing his way along her jaw to that spot behind her ear that made her shiver. "Mmm. Good. So good."

"Yes. It is. It was." *Close call.* She shoved against

his arms, shifting back a few inches. How could he never have known? How could he never have guessed? She'd thought there'd been something between them, something… "It's also getting late," she said.

He raised his head to stare at her, blinking as though she'd thrown a switch on a spotlight and aimed it his way.

"I think this was a mistake," she said.

"You do?" he asked, still blinking.

"Don't you?"

"I'm not sure." His gaze dropped to her mouth. "Let's try it again."

"Dev—"

"Yes, yes," he murmured, drawing her in again. "I'm right here."

"Yes, you are."

"Where else did you think I'd be?" he asked with a smile.

"Well, I—" She sighed against his mouth as he dropped another of his soft, sweet kisses on hers. Yes, he was here…for now. But he'd be gone by the end of summer. Or sooner, if he got bored. Bored with life here in the Cove. With her. "Never mind."

He rested his forehead against hers. "Moment over?"

She blew out the breath she hadn't realized she'd been holding. And then she straightened, nodded and patted his chest—his broad, warm chest—before backing out of his embrace. "Moment over."

He slid his hands into his pockets. "At least I got my grinding done."

She smiled weakly at the thought of the grinding that had taken place. "Yes," she said, gesturing lamely in the direction of his project. "And it turned out really well."

She groaned and shut her eyes. When she opened them, he was grinning at her. "You told Teddi hers was great," he said.

"Yours is great, too."

"You told Virgil he has a knack for it."

"Yes," she said, nodding. Considering. Teasing Dev with a smile. "I did."

"Okay, then." He pulled his car keys from his pocket and stared at them, frowning. "What comes next, anyway? After the caming and soldering?"

"Glazing."

"Is that easier than grinding?"

"Messier. Bring Rosie with you."

"That bad, huh?"

"No." She headed toward her door to unlock it for him. "But it's something she could help you with."

"And then…we're finished."

"That's right," she said as she turned to face him.

"Class over."

"Yep."

"Are you going to offer any other stained-glass classes this summer?" He cocked his head to one side. "Mosaics, for instance?"

She rested one hand on the doorknob and the other on her hip. "Good night, Dev."

"You know, I've been rethinking that whole friend-ship thing." He sauntered toward the exit and then paused a few feet away. "I can't figure out why we've never given it a shot. I've always liked you, you know."

"That's nice to hear." His casual tone helped her nerves smooth back into normal range. "I've always liked you, too."

"I figured. You were just too stubborn to admit it."

"Maybe I was waiting for you to say it first." She opened her door and leaned against the jamb. "Good night, Dev."

"I don't suppose you—"

"Good night, Dev."

"Right." He stepped through her doorway. "By the way, I also like the way you teach."

Her cheeks flamed like torches, and she was certain they'd spontaneously combust at some point if she didn't get rid of him. "Good night, Dev."

"Yeah." He gave her a smile that sizzled through the rest of her, too. "It is."

DEV STEPPED THROUGH Tess's office door Wednesday morning, carrying one of the syrupy, flavored coffees she drank as if they were the elixir of life. "Morning."

His cousin glanced up from her computer monitor. "What are you doing here?"

"Bringing you this." He set the takeout cup on the edge of her desk and dropped into her apple-red visitor's chair.

"Is it a bribe?" She sniffed suspiciously before sipping. "Should I be searching for ulterior motives in the mocha?"

"Were you always this cynical?"

"Were you always this calculating?"

He shrugged at the possibility and swallowed some of his plain black brew. "What's that?" he asked, gesturing with his cup toward her screen.

"The floor plan for a suite of medical offices." She manipulated the mouse and added another line to the plan. "Dr. Samuels. Remember him?"

"Is he still alive?"

"And kicking. Just brought in young Dr. Samuels as his new partner, and this—" she nodded at the screen "—is going to be their new place."

"Georgie Samuels? All-county quarterback Georgie Samuels?"

"One and the same."

"Wow."

"Scary, huh?" Tess shuddered. "Wouldn't want young Dr. Samuels throwing a pass in my direction now."

"Wouldn't think he'd try."

"He did, once." She swiveled in her chair, a cat-got-the-canary smile on her face. "The summer before my senior year."

"Please. Spare me the details." Dev drained the last of his coffee and pitched the cup into Tess's stylish waste bin. "Do you use accounting software?"

"Of course."

She minimized the plan on her screen and tapped a few keys as he moved to stand behind her, leaning over her shoulder to view the display. "Is this research for one of your stories?" she asked.

"I don't know yet. Depends on what I find out." He noted the name of the software when it opened—the same he'd seen on the papers in Geneva's files. "How long have you been using this program?"

"Less than a year. Since I opened my business."

"So you wouldn't know about upgrades."

"Upgrades." She shuddered. "Don't say that word out loud. You'll draw the attention of the evil nerd spirits."

"Would you know if certain functions are stable from one version to the next?"

"There are functions I've never looked at. We have an understanding—I don't poke around where I don't belong, and this thing doesn't wipe out my invoices." She tapped another key and another set of columns appeared. "What is it you're looking for?"

"The audit trail."

Tess pointed to an item on the menu bar and selected it to show a cascade of choices on the screen. "See here? 'Audit trail.' Clicking this item—turning this off—is a very big no-no, my accountant tells me. One of the seven deadly bookkeeping sins, along with losing receipts and forgetting to back up your records—not that I've ever been guilty of either of those, you understand."

Dev grinned. "Of course not."

"On the other hand," Tess said as she wiggled the cursor away from the dangerous spot, "could be a handy plot device if a mystery writer were working on a story about embezz—"

She froze and then slowly turned to face him. "You wouldn't dare," she whispered. "You wouldn't dare do that to Addie. Or to her mother."

"I'm not trying to do anything to anyone." He leaned forward, studying the screen. "At this point, I'm simply trying to understand what happened."

"There's nothing to 'understand.' Lena was accused of embezzlement. Geneva refused to bring charges. Case dropped. It's a matter of record. Knowing why won't change the facts."

"I'm going to find out."

"There aren't enough mochas in the known universe to convince me to help you dredge all this up again." She pressed a couple of keys, and her monitor screen went dark. "Leave them in peace."

"A peace that's left them in limbo?"

"That's not for you to decide."

"My father was involved in this, too."

"He's dead. Sorry, Dev," Tess added, cringing, "but he can't be hurt by this. Not anymore."

Dev dropped his hands to her shoulders and gave her an affectionate squeeze. "It's going to be okay."

"You're going to hurt her."

"No. I won't."

"You can't help it. And when you leave, she'll be hurt again."

"I'm not going anywhere." He headed toward the door. "I told you—I'm sticking around until the end of summer."

"Oh, great. That'll make everything so much better." Tess leaned her elbows on her desk and buried her face in her hands. "I've got months of anxiety to look forward to."

"You'll get over it." He opened her door and turned to face her. "I'm not going to turn my back on the past or run off to the city when the going gets tough. Not anymore."

CHAPTER FIFTEEN

"WHY, DEV," ADDIE SAID as Rosie lifted the neck strap of one of Tess's frilliest aprons over his head on Thursday afternoon. "I never would have guessed pink would be such a good color on you."

The scorching glance he sent her was a potent reminder of what had happened after class two days ago.

You've never been kissed by me.

And when summer ended, she'd probably never be kissed like that again. Dev would be gone in a few weeks, and until that time, she intended to kiss him every chance she got. To store up memories to stash beside her fantasies. Memories of fiery, bold, primary-color kisses that put her muted pastel dreams to shame.

Hold on tight.

"Let me get that for you, Virgil." Addie moved around the table to tie a string bow at the back of Virgil's waist. "Looks like this apron has seen its share of barbecues."

"When I put on an apron, I don't mess around." Virgil adjusted the band around his neck and stepped back, arms raised. "Good enough for the goo?"

Addie nodded. "Good enough. Is everyone ready?"

"I guess so." Teddi stared at her container of black

glazier's putty with obvious revulsion. "Are you sure that stuff we rubbed on our hands will keep them clean?"

Addie held up her own. "You never see any black on mine, do you?" She scooped half a handful of the putty onto a paper plate and pressed her thumb in the middle to make a shallow well. "Okay, dig in. Get your putty on your work area, and I'll come around with the oil."

Rosie plunged her hand into Dev's container and scraped up the right amount of oily black goo. *"Awesome."*

"Good job." Addie added a bit of linseed oil to Rosie's putty. "Now knead it like a little loaf of bread."

"What's kneading?"

"I'll show you." Dev folded the putty, pressed with the heel of his hand and then flipped over another fold to press again.

Addie stared, amazed. "You bake?"

"No." His smile was a slow, stroking tease. "I dated a baker once."

Addie stared at his hands as they squeezed and pressed and massaged the black goo, and she imagined the feel of those hands moving over her skin as she kissed him.

"Let me do it." Rosie took over the chore, and Addie moved around the table, checking on her students' progress.

In another hour or two, they'd all be finished. They'd shove the putty into the came, sprinkle whiting over the mess, scrub with stiff brushes, cut the putty from the edges and vacuum it all away. By the time they'd buffed their projects with steel wool and vacuumed a second time, they'd see the beautiful results of all their hard work.

And then her first leaded-glass class would be over. She'd learned a lot from the experience—including the fact that she didn't want to repeat it anytime soon. The extra cash was nice, but she hadn't realized how exhausted she'd be at the end of each class day.

"I had no idea so many steps went into making a stained-glass window." Barb shook her head. "I have new respect for the time that must have gone into all these pieces in your shop, Addie."

"You'd get faster with practice," Addie told her. "But it's not the easiest craft to learn. And you've all done very well."

"Even Dev," Rosie said.

"Even Dev." Addie shared a secret smile with him. He'd arrived when the shop opened that morning, marched to the work area behind her counter and labored diligently—and with little assistance—to apply the came to his pieces and catch up with the others.

He'd been a good sport, considering all the teasing he'd taken. And he'd been amazingly patient, considering he'd signed up for all the wrong reasons.

He nudged Rosie, nearly knocking her off her stool, and she grinned and nudged him back. He was a good sport with ten-year-old pests, too.

Addie made one more circuit of the table, checking the consistency of everyone's putty, and then demonstrated how to apply it to the edges of the came. "Be sure and stick it against every bit of lead. Don't worry about working it in—we'll do that next. Just get a good amount of it stuck along those edges."

Because Dev and Rosie worked as a team, they finished long before the others. "May I wash my hands now?" Dev asked.

"Go ahead. I'm sure Rosie can handle the messy parts from here on out."

"All right." Rosie grinned. "This is definitely the best part."

"I thought you'd enjoy it."

Addie crossed to the grinder bench and reached beneath it to haul her shop vacuum from its storage spot.

"Let me get that for you," Dev said, placing a hand on her back and leaning over her. "You smell like linseed oil," he murmured in her ear.

She froze, hoping that none of the other students would notice the way he'd moved in close, trapping her beneath him. "It's cheaper than perfume," she whispered.

"And every bit as sexy."

She grabbed the hose and tugged it loose, hitting Dev in the stomach with the nozzle. He backed out of her way and into the path of the fat canister. One of its wheels bumped over the toe of his scruffy sports shoe.

"Is that the kind of things friends notice?" she asked.

"Certain kinds of friends," he answered with a smug grin, rubbing his midsection. He looped the hose back over the top of the machine and dragged it to the work-table.

The bell over her front door jangled, and she moved into her shop area to help a customer choose mosaic tiles. She glanced over her shoulder to see Dev browsing through the cutter selection.

"What are you doing out here?" she asked after her customer had left.

"Am I going to get detention?"

"You're supposed to be supervising Rosie."

"She promised she wouldn't eat the steel wool or drown herself in the bathroom." Dev shrugged. "I figured she'd be okay on her own for a couple of minutes."

"Do you trust her with Barb?"

He craned his neck to peer past the display shelves. "She hasn't drowned Barb in the bathroom, either."

"What do you want?"

"To treat you to dinner tonight. As a thank you. For letting me come in early and take up your entire day."

"It wasn't any trouble."

"Then let me treat you just because. How about takeout?" he added when she hesitated. "We could eat here, if you'd like."

He'd always had a talent for making it impossible to say no. And she'd waited so long to be able to say yes.

Yes, Dev. *Yes.*

"Yes," she told him, her fingers spread over the flutters in her stomach. "I'd love to."

ADDIE WAVED GOODBYE to Virgil as he pulled his truck from the curb outside her shop. Teddi and Barb had left earlier, with proud smiles on their faces and beautiful stained-glass pictures in their hands. Shortly after they'd gone, Dev had walked Rosie around the corner to Tess's office, promising to return with dinner.

Addie flipped her shop sign to Closed. She turned off the lights and stood alone in the welcome silence, soaking up the peace. She supposed she'd miss the chatter and activity in her work area during the coming weeks, but it would be nice to have the space back to herself.

She had a major repair job to finish.

A knock on her door interrupted her thoughts. Outside, a mustached gentleman dressed in a waiter's formal black-and-white suit stood holding an armful of snowy white linens.

She opened her door. "Yes?"

"Takeout dinner delivery for Signorina Sutton. From Amalfi."

Amalfi—the most expensive Italian restaurant in town. Stunned, she stepped aside as he entered her shop. He was quickly followed by two other men, one of them in a chef's double-breasted white jacket and toque.

"Where may we set your table, *signorina?*" asked Mr. Mustache.

"Back here." She led the way through the shop, past the counter and into the work area. Opening her apartment door, she gestured toward the small, round table in the center of her living space. "I hope this will do."

"Perfectly. *Grazie.*" Mr. Mustache lifted the centerpiece of drooping roses from the table and handed it to her with a fussy little bow, and then he flapped one of the linens into the air like a sail, settling it theatrically over her table. Candles, flowers, crystal, a silver bucket of ice and sparkling place settings quickly followed.

This couldn't be happening. Things like this—beautiful, extravagant, romantic things—didn't happen to her.

"Hi."

Addie turned to find Dev slouched in her apartment doorway, one shoulder against the jamb and his hands in his pockets. "Pizza okay?" he asked.

She nodded, speechless.

Mr. Mustache lit the candles. The chef whisked silver domes from trays of artistically presented antipasto, chocolate-drizzled cannoli and two small pizzas. The sommelier showed Dev two bottles of wine for his approval and then they all trooped out. Dev followed, and Addie heard the click of her shop door lock.

"What is all this?" she asked when he returned.

"A takeout dinner."

"This isn't takeout." Her words spilled out in a high-pitched, panicky rasp, and she swallowed to clear her throat. "Well, I suppose it is, technically, but—"

"Addie." He walked slowly toward her, lifted one of her hands to his mouth and brushed a kiss across her knuckles. His hot, dark gaze kicked her pulse into overdrive.

"What was that?" she asked as she tried to tug her hand free. He couldn't be doing this, not to her.

"A thank-you kiss." He drew her toward the tiny galley kitchen arranged along one of the side walls. "We should wash our hands before dinner."

He twisted the old porcelain tap, and she moved in to hold a palm beneath the water that flowed into the deep farmhouse sink, checking the temperature. He shifted behind her, crowding her against the counter, encircling her within his arms as he reached for the soap.

His body pressed along her length, one of his knees rubbing the back of one of hers, and his breath puffed warmly against the side of her neck. He took her hands in his and began to soap them. Slowly, slickly, he laced his fingers with hers and squeezed. "I love the way your soap smells," he murmured against her hair.

She was grateful for the support of the counter. She wasn't sure she could remain standing on her rubbery knees. "It's lemon."

"When I smell citrus, it makes me think of you." He nuzzled a sensitive spot at the base of her shoulder, and his end-of-the-day whiskers tickled the side of her neck. "Where's your towel?"

"What?"

"Your towel." He nipped at her earlobe, sending shivers in a cascade down her spine.

"Here." With trembling, clumsy fingers she pulled the checkerboard-print cloth from its hook near her plate rack and quickly scrubbed it over her hands before handing it to him.

He moved to the table and lifted one of the bottles. "Would you like a glass of wine?"

She pressed a hand against her stomach, wondering if a drink would calm her jitters. And wondering if she'd be too relaxed to deal with him. "Yes, thank you," she answered. "Thank you."

He poured red wine into two goblets and handed one to her. "Here's to the end of my first—and most likely my last—stained-glass class. And to my beautiful teacher." He touched his glass to hers with a quiet clink and stared at her with that same unnerving intensity as he sipped.

She tasted the wine, its rich, fruity flavor blooming in a potent, delicious, glorious bouquet. This was nothing like other red wines she'd sampled, and she suspected the vintage Dev had chosen was more expensive than those she'd tried in the past.

He strolled toward her cramped sitting area, stepping onto the threadbare area rug that defined the space. "Do you mind giving me a short tour?" he asked. He leaned over her sagging love seat to study the wine-country print hanging on the brick wall above it. "I have to admit, I've been curious about what was behind these curtains."

She did a quick mental inventory of the state of the area behind the screen. Dirty clothes in their basket instead of draped over the chair, underwear in the drawers instead of dripping from the line in the bath. Dilly had probably dived beneath the unmade bed when the staff from Amalfi had walked in, but she couldn't trust her naughty cat to stay undercover for long if there was food to tempt him out of hiding.

"It'll have to be a short tour," she said as she recovered the food, "since it's really just one room. Well, sort of."

She took a larger, fortifying sip and joined him in front of the sofa. "Tess gave me this print years ago, after her mother opened the gallery in the city. It's one of my favorites. One of her father's paintings. Your uncle's." Odd that she hadn't made the connection until that moment.

"Yes, I know." He stared at it for another few seconds. "The original is hanging in my apartment in San Francisco."

"It is?"

"Tess doesn't know. No one in the family knows, I'm sure. Unless the gallery assistant who sold it to me told Aunt Jacqueline." He sipped his wine. "It's always been one of my favorites, too."

Addie was beginning to realize she didn't know Dev as well as she'd always thought. How many other secrets did he have? "And this," she said, "completes the tour of the living room, dining room and kitchen."

"I like it." He grinned and skimmed a finger from her shoulder to her wrist in a tingling path. And then he wrapped his hand around hers—a warm, solid weight at the end of her arm—and gave it a soft squeeze.

The simple, affectionate gesture moved her more than any of his seductive touches or smoky glances, and an elemental cadence began to throb deep inside her. *Dev, Dev.* It was happening again—the same impossible yearning, the same overwhelming temptation. He wanted her, tonight. He was making it clear in hundreds of ways. And she wanted him, too. In hundreds of ways. She wouldn't be able to resist him, not tonight.

She'd probably be sorry in the morning. But there was a chance she'd be sorrier still if she never shared this night with him. If this was all she could have— these few days, these few weeks with him—then she should take as much as she could get.

She shifted her hand, turning her palm up to lace her fingers through his, and squeezed back.

He shifted closer, leaning in to place another kiss along her jaw, and she moved her head to the side so he'd linger. "What's next?" he murmured.

"Everything behind the screen." She led him around the edge of the folding wooden frame and gestured with her goblet at her bedroom area. "The dresser. The armoire—standing in for the missing closet. The trunk that holds everything that won't fit anywhere else. The bathroom, behind that plywood wall."

"And the tub." He let go of her hand to skirt the foot

of her bed and stare at the claw-foot tub angled across one corner of the room. Old-fashioned plumbing rose to shower height and formed one section of a ring supporting a plain white curtain. "Cool."

"Yes." She finished her wine and set her glass on her nightstand. "Very cool, after about fifteen minutes, when the hot water runs out."

"And this is the bed," he said.

"Yes." She raised her hand to her neckline and unfastened one button with trembling fingers. "And this is the end of the tour."

He emptied his glass, lowered it to the stack of old crates in the corner and stood, staring at her across the expanse of rumpled quilts. She recognized the reflection of her own nerves in his jerky swallow and flickering gaze, and the thought that she'd unsettled him gave her the reckless courage to undo another button.

"What about dinner?" he asked, staring at the gap in her shirt.

"Are you hungry?"

She reached up to unfasten one of the clips in her hair, and he lifted his hands, palms out.

"Stop," he said. "Just…*stop*."

She froze, gripping a plastic butterfly, iced through with mortification. She'd known she'd be clumsy at this. She'd never seduced a man before, and it had been a major mistake to try the trick now, when every move, every word, mattered so very much.

Dev moved around the bed and pried her fingers from the clip. "Let me do that," he whispered.

CHAPTER SIXTEEN

DEV HAD INTENDED TO take things slow. He'd meant to savor every moment of this first time with Addie—had made big plans for a memorable scene—but his hands were shaking, and his knees were knocking, and his breath was backing up in his lungs. He was afraid she'd drive him stark, raving mad with her innocent striptease. There was only so much a man could take.

"I love your hair," he said as he pulled out the clips. He shoved his hands along her scalp and combed his fingers through to the ends. "Promise you'll never cut it."

"I have to keep it trimmed. And besides," she added, frowning, "that's not your decision to make."

"You're right." He framed her face in his hands and pressed a soft kiss to her forehead. "I lost my head." And another to her cheek. "I can get a little crazy—" and another to the tip of her nose "—on home tours. Especially when there are antiques involved."

"Do you like antiques?"

"Yes." He slid his hands down her shoulders and reached for the next button on her shirt. "Very much."

He worked his way down, grazing her stomach with his knuckles and smiling at her shivers, until he slid the last button through the last hole. He swept her shirt over her shoulders and down to the floor. "Beautiful," he murmured, tracing the edges of her bra with his fingertips, teasing her with touches that meandered over cotton and lace and skin. "I knew you'd be beautiful."

"Dev."

"Hmm?"

"The bed's an antique."

He grinned. "That sound you just heard was my control snapping."

He tugged the hem of his shirt over his head, and her hands streaked over his chest, grasping and kneading before he'd untangled his arms from the sleeves. He drew her against him, desperate for the feel of flesh against flesh, and she wrapped her arms around his neck, giving him what he wanted. He tipped her to the side, and she took him with her, and they laughed when they fell with a bounce onto her bed.

She scrambled over him, straddling his hips, and raised her arms like a pagan goddess to lift her hair above her head. And then she leaned forward, letting it fall in a silky curtain around his face as he cupped her breasts in his hands. "Beautiful," he said. *"Addie."*

Her busy hands attacked the fastenings at the front of his jeans, and he arched up, knocking her to the side, to tug a foil packet from his back pocket. She rolled back into his arms, and he crushed her lips with his, sinking into a mindless pleasure. Hands stroked, teeth nipped and someone—he thought it might have been him—groaned.

"Let's get inside," she murmured against his mouth in her siren's voice.

"That's the plan."

"I meant inside the sheets."

"That'll work, too."

They scooted off her rumpled quilt, drew back the layers of covers and shimmied out of their pants in a frantic race. She kicked off her sandals, and he hopped on one foot, wrestling with one of his shoes and nearly knocking over her nightstand when he lost his balance. "Remind me to buy a pair of flip-flops," he said as he climbed into bed with her and pulled the sheet over their bodies.

"I forgot to get a good look," he said after she'd snuggled close again.

"That'll teach you."

"I knew you'd figure out a way to give me detention." He shifted to sprawl over her. "Guess I'll just have to find my way by feel."

She smiled as she lifted her hands to cradle his face. "That'll work, too."

"Addie." He lowered his head, trying to show her with one kiss what this night meant to him. "There's so much I want to say."

"I know." She raised a knee, rubbing her soft foot along his leg. "I feel the same way." She trailed her fingers up and down his spine. "I thought I'd be shy with you, but I'm not."

"Was it the dinner?" He brushed his lips over one perfect, rosy nipple. "The candlelight?" He ran his tongue around the other one. "The wine?"

She gasped and shook her head. "No. It was when you finished your project and turned it over, and there was a piece of paper still stuck to one of your glass pieces."

He stilled. "Is this your new method of leveling the playing field?"

Her soft laugh was a warm vibration beneath his chest. He covered her mouth with his and began to concentrate on the serious part of the evening. Yes, he had a lot to say, with the glide of his hand down her back and the stroke of his tongue along her lips. And she answered, with a soft sigh of surrender and a flowing ripple of delight.

Somewhere outside, a siren wailed through the night, and the evening shadows grew together into darkness as her mantel clock ticked off the seconds. Her pillows smelled of flowers, like her hair, and she tasted of wine and womanly secrets. He breathed deeply, and tasted deeply, and still couldn't get his fill of the woman in his arms. He suspected he never would.

Everything between them tonight seemed new and fresh, and yet somehow part of an old, familiar pattern. They rubbed along together, searching and exploring and straining for their perfect fit, their own click of connection. He slid inside her, as easy as an old friend and as fervent as a new lover. She arched up, taking him deeper, welcoming him in, welcoming him home.

So good, so right.

ADDIE SAT ACROSS FROM Dev on her bed near midnight, both of them cross-legged and partially wrapped in her sheet. They'd feasted on the antipasto—sharing a few bites with Dilly—and reminisced about school days and summer vacations. She'd told him about her desire to travel, and he'd told her about some of the places he'd seen. And then they'd made love again, a fast, plunging roller coaster of pleasure and joy that had left them tangled in the quilts, laughing and breathless and sated…for the moment.

She finished her second slice of pizza and began to lick her fingers clean.

"Here," Dev said, pulling her hand to his mouth. "Let me get that for you." He sucked on her fingers, tickling them with his tongue. And then he kissed her fingertips, her palm and her wrist before shoving her hand back into her lap and taking another bite of his own pizza slice.

She smiled and grabbed the second bottle from the bucket propped on the mattress. "More?"

He reached behind him to retrieve his goblet from the nightstand, and she dribbled the rest of the wine into his glass. "I wish we could have been together," she said. "Before, when we were in school."

"Like this?" He frowned. "We were kids. We still had a lot of growing up to do—I did, anyway." He gave her one of his long-lashed gazes, the thoughtful kind of expression that was on her list of top-ten favorites. "We might have ruined what we have now."

She rested her elbows on her knees and folded her hands beneath her chin, cherishing the fact that they had a *now* to share. And that Dev could shift so easily from passion to philosophy and back again. He was an endlessly fascinating man. "Or we might have skipped all the lost times in between," she said.

He shrugged and took another bite. "We'll never know."

She sighed and stretched out on her side, facing him. "I don't mind not knowing."

"You don't?"

"Does that surprise you?"

"Nothing about you surprises me anymore." He carefully scooped the rest of their things into the bucket, placed it on the floor and crawled across the bed to sprawl over her in his artless, effective way.

"Now there's a phrase with more than one interpretation," she said as she stroked his hair from his eyes.

"We could discuss the possibilities in a different location." He dropped one of his sweet kisses on the tip of her nose. "Want to find out whether that tub of yours is big enough for two?"

AS DAWN ADDED TRACES of pastel to the gray shadows in Addie's room on Friday, Dev lay beside her, his chin in his hand, watching her sleep. He'd considered waking her an hour ago for one last, leisurely round of lovemaking, but he'd decided she needed her rest. She had a full day of work ahead of her. And they'd had a very busy night.

And he was content to lie here, watching her. For the first time in his life, he hadn't awakened with restless dissatisfaction with what he had to do that day or where he happened to be at that moment. He was exactly where he wanted to be and doing exactly what he'd always been meant to do—loving Addie Sutton.

The process of falling for her had been so gradual he couldn't have seen it if he'd looked. And so inevitable he couldn't have escaped it if he'd tried. As simple as breathing, as difficult as life could sometimes be. From the moment he'd first seen the fascinating little girl to the moment he'd finally taken the bewitching woman into his arms—every moment had been leading to the next. To this one, here, with her. To love.

Nothing part-time for Dev Chandler anymore, he thought with a stupid, sappy grin. He'd talk with Geneva about a long-term stay in her guest house, and he'd start looking for a job here in the Cove. He didn't need the money, but he needed to be a permanent part of the place.

The room lightened another degree, and he skimmed a finger down the miniature ski slope of Addie's nose.

"Mmph." She moaned and rubbed her nose, opening her eyes. "What? What are you doing?"

"Waking you up." He shifted closer, tossing his leg over hers, and she snuggled against him, all warm and pillowy. "I should go soon," he said. "My car's still parked out in front of your shop."

She stiffened. "I don't suppose there's any point in worrying about that now?"

"Probably not."

She rolled onto her back with a sigh and stared at her ceiling. "I'm awake now."

"Good. Because there's something I want to ask you."

"Out to breakfast?"

"Sorry." He combed his fingers through her hair, arranging it over her pillow. "I have to drive out to the bluff to take care of Geneva's dogs."

"And I should clean up my shop and get ready for work."

"Okay, then." He paused, trying to swallow. Asking a girl for a date shouldn't dry up all his spit like this—especially when he was in bed with her. "There's this dance on Saturday night. I want you to come with me."

The look of shock on her face nearly made him wince. "Are you asking me out?"

"I thought we could give it a try." He lifted a

shoulder in a casual shrug. "If it works, we could go steady."

"We're not—"

"Friends? Lovers? A couple?" He leaned forward and pressed a soft kiss to her lips. And another, just because he could—and to prove his point. "Maybe it's time to make some changes."

She smiled and slid a hand behind his head, pulling him close for a kiss of her own. "Maybe we should take things one step at a time."

"We're doing okay so far, aren't we?" He traced her lower lip with a finger. "Besides, we won't know unless we give it a shot."

"All right. I'd love to go out with you on Saturday night." She smiled and nipped at his fingertip. "Where's the dance?"

"At The Breakers."

She stiffened again.

"It's the anniversary dance," he said. "Not a ball, really, but—"

"Very dressy."

"Yeah. Kind of." He hadn't packed a suit, he realized with a frown. He hoped he could find one on short notice.

He shoved his way through the tangle of quilts on her bed and grabbed his jeans from the floor. And then he leaned back to take her in his arms and kiss her some more because he still couldn't get enough of her, although he sure enjoyed trying to. "Addie?"

"Yes?"

"Remember when I said last night that nothing you do surprises me anymore?"

"Yes."

"I was wrong." He kissed her again. "You snore."

DEV RAISED A HAND in greeting Friday afternoon as Geneva strode across the tarmac with the other shuttle passengers, heading toward the tiny airport's arrival gate. She adjusted the shoulder strap on her tote and responded with a smile. She looked happy and rested, he noted as she drew near. And he was incredibly happy to see her.

But then, he was incredibly happy with everything today.

He moved to one side of the small patio cordoned off from the tarmac with a low chain-link fence and waited until she'd passed through the gate. And then he stepped forward, wrapped his arms around her and hugged her tightly, lifting her off the ground and swinging her in a circle.

"Well." She wrestled a smile under control and patted her hair, after he'd set her down, though he'd come nowhere near to mussing her upswept roll. "You certainly seem to be in high spirits this afternoon."

"Sorry about the PDA."

"I beg your pardon?"

"Public display of affection."

She smiled. "I think I like that acronym."

"Want another?"

She laughed and took his arm. "And here I thought you'd be growling after having been forced to spend time with my dogs."

"They aren't so bad."

"Not when someone else is looking after them, you mean."

He grinned. "I should have known you'd check up on me."

"Yes, you should have."

They followed the other passengers through a door into a narrow reception area. At one end, a short luggage carousel belt began a rumbling turn through the room and out again.

"I remember when they used to set our luggage on a bicycle rack near that same spot." Geneva smiled. "This is one more improvement Carnelian Cove can boast of."

"You love it here," he said.

"I have since I first saw this place." She searched his face. "You love it, too. Even though you're always in a hurry to leave."

"Yeah." He glanced at the wall behind her—a mural of a fanciful Victorian farmhouse tucked beneath a redwood grove, dark ocean cliffs and white foamy waves in the background. "It's a special place."

"So it's not the place you're escaping. It's the people."

"Is that one of your bags?" At her nod, he squeezed past the small knot of passengers to lift it from the belt, glad he'd had an excuse to avoid answering her question. How could he make her understand he'd been escaping himself, too? Escaping his inability to earn his father's notice, escaping his forbidden attraction to Addie.

A matching case soon appeared, and he collected that, too. "Is this all?" he asked.

"Yes." She handed him her tote, and he stacked it on a case and looped the strap around the handle. "I also shipped a few things home," she said.

"I knew there'd be more." He gently nudged her with his elbow. "I know how much you like to shop."

"You seem to enjoy the things I buy for you."

"Not complaining," he said with a grin, "just saying."

He led the way to her car, which he'd parked near the exit, and opened her door before loading her things in the trunk.

"I heard you've developed an interest in stained glass," Geneva said after he'd pulled out on the highway.

"Should have kept that interest strictly academic." He shook his head. "I am, according to Rosie, a 'total loser' at the craft."

"Does Addie share her opinion?"

"I'm sure she does. But she's too smart to tell a prospective client that he has no business handling the stuff."

"You seem to admire her a great deal," Geneva said.

"Addie?"

"You know very well who we were discussing."

"You were discussing her." Dev struggled to keep a grin off his face. It wasn't often he got the upper hand in a battle of wits with his grandmother. "I was talking about craft classes."

Geneva's eyes narrowed as she stared at him, and he could practically hear the wheels turning in her devious mind. He knew he'd soften and tell her what she wanted to hear. In part, because his grandmother had given him one of the many shoves he'd needed to get him to this place: madly, passionately, completely in love with a woman who'd always been here, in his true home, waiting for him as he traveled the world looking for her.

"Okay, then," he said at last. "We can talk about Addie. I'll start by pointing out that the last thing you said to me before you left—after all your fussing about walking your dogs, and collecting the newspapers and keeping the kitchen clean—was that you wanted me to realize I'm not seventeen anymore."

He gave his grandmother a smile filled with everything that was in his heart. "I'm happy to report that I followed all your instructions. To the letter."

"I'm happy to hear it. And Addie?"

"Is my date to the anniversary dance at The Breakers tomorrow night."

"Well." Geneva relaxed against her seat, her posture declaring mission accomplished. "That PDA was a nice welcome home. But this news is even better."

She rested a hand on his arm, a personal display of affection. "Welcome home to you, too, Dev."

LOCKING HER SHOP DOOR shortly after closing on Friday night, Addie fumbled as she tried to pull her ringing cell phone from her purse. "Yes?"

"Charlie's here," Tess said. "Are you on your way?"

"As soon as I get off this phone and into my truck."

"Relax. We've got everything under control."

Which is why Addie had called her friends in a panic that morning. She needed a dress—heck, she needed everything. Shoes, jewelry, a handbag, perfume, makeup. A makeover, she thought as she climbed into her truck and caught a glimpse of her reflection in her rearview mirror.

She took another minute to stare. The bags beneath her eyes couldn't disguise their cat-that-got-the-cream shine. Tess and Charlie would take one look at her face and know exactly what had happened the night before.

No way, Addie laughed as she backed out of her

alley parking space, giddy with the memories of what she'd shared with Dev throughout the night. Her friends had great imaginations, but they'd never come close. Addie's own fantasies hadn't come close.

She drove east, toward the newer subdivisions along the river. An evening breeze ruffled the delicate foliage of the redwoods hanging over the winding road, and the charcoal scent of a backyard barbecue drifted through her open window.

At this time tomorrow night, she'd be out on a date with Dev Chandler. At The Breakers Golf and Country Club.

"I don't believe it," she said and laughed out loud. It was like prom, for adults. Competitive dressing, intense scrutiny of every detail. She'd need to make an appointment for a pedicure—and then find the time to keep it.

Tess opened her front door before Addie had a chance to lift the silly tortoise-shaped knocker. "We've already decided what you should wear," she said as she yanked Addie inside. "All we need from you is your official okay."

Her friend's announcement didn't do anything to lower Addie's stress level. "I don't have a say in this?" she asked as Tess dragged her down the hall to her bright blue bedroom.

"About the dress?" Tess paused in the doorway. "Or about how you're going to pay us back?"

Addie frowned as she moved past Tess and entered the room. "I asked if I could borrow a dress. I didn't ask you to…*oh*." She staggered to a stop and stared at the cloudlike dream of a dress spread over Tess's quilted spread. "Oh, my."

"Isn't it perfect?" Charlie ran a hand along the

frothy hem. Thin, sparkling straps supported a silver-beaded bodice cinched with a softly pleated chiffon sash. A floaty skirt of the same whispery fabric fell in darker, ruffling layers like curling smoke.

Addie shook her head. "I can't possibly afford this."

"We can," Charlie said.

"But I can't pay you back."

"That's what you think." Tess lifted the dress and held it against Addie. "Gorgeous. I knew it would be. Perfect for the club and for the occasion. Perfect with your coloring."

"It is perfect. Thank you. Oh, I love it." Addie spread her hands over her midsection to hold the fabulous outift against her faded cotton camp shirt. "But a true friend wouldn't take advantage of my desperation."

"Girlfriend, you don't know what true desperation is." Tess held one of the sparkly straps against Addie's shoulder, her head cocked to one side. "You owe me one slumber-party overnight chaperoning Rosie and the friend of her choice."

Addie caught a glimpse of her reflection in Tess's mirror. "Deal."

"I'm thinking we'll do your eyes in smudgy grey, make them look even bigger than they are." Tess spread the dress over her bed again and pulled a handful of brushes and tubes from a quilted satin sack. "Glossy lips. Mauve, maybe. Something translucent on your nails."

Addie shoved her hands behind her back. "Not my hands."

"You've got to have a manicure. And a pedicure," Tess added, glancing at Addie's toes. "You'll need some strappy shoes, too. Heels would be best, but you don't want to break an ankle dancing."

"I don't have any strappy shoes."

"That's tomorrow's chore. Along with the appointment at the salon."

Addie turned to the one woman she knew would understand. *"Charlie."*

"Don't ask me for help," Charlie warned. "She's already scheduled a torture session for me before my wedding."

"And what do I owe you for your share in this?" Addie asked Charlie.

"I'll think of something."

"I can't agree to those terms." Addie ran a finger along one of the ripply chiffon layers. "But this dress…"

"Try it on." Tess passed it to Addie. "I want to see it on you. All that blond hair tumbling down in the back—"

"I thought you said she'd have to wear it up." Charlie frowned. "I thought you said—"

"I said a lot of things. I'm allowed to change my mind. First, the dress." Tess's lips curled up in one of her witchy smiles. "Then we'll argue about the rest."

CHAPTER SEVENTEEN

DEV CARRIED A PLATE heaped with Julia's pancakes into the breakfast room at Chandler House shortly after seven on Saturday morning. He placed a hand on Geneva's shoulder, gave her a quick kiss on her cheek and slipped into the seat across from hers.

"I'm speechless." Geneva stared as he poured himself a cup of coffee. "Absolutely speechless."

He spread a napkin in his lap and grinned. He hadn't put in a breakfast appearance since he'd graduated from high school. Setting his alarm for half-past dawn this morning had been worth seeing the delighted shock on her face. "You could start with 'Good morning, Dev,'" he suggested.

"All right, then." She lifted her coffee, sipped, set her cup aside. "Good morning, Dev."

"Good morning, Grandmother." He settled more comfortably in his chair, stretching his legs beneath the table. "How did you sleep?"

"Much better than I did while I was away."

"That's one of the best things about travel." He poured warm syrup over his stack and cut the first wedge-shaped bite. "Coming home."

"Yes, it is." Geneva cocked her head to one side. "And did you sleep well, Dev?"

"I slept alone, if that's what you're asking."

"I'm not about to pry into your personal affairs, if that's what you're volunteering." Geneva's lips curved in a hopeful smile as she spooned a dab of marmalade onto a slice of toast. "Is it?"

"No."

"I thought as much." She lifted her fork and poked at her omelet. "Well, then. Out with it."

He swallowed another mouthful of pancakes and took a sip of coffee to wash them down. "You never pressed charges against Lena Sutton."

"No."

The challenge on Geneva's face made him reconsider his next question. He wanted answers this morning, not clever obstructions. "So she never got the chance to clear herself of any suspicion," he said.

"I didn't suspect her." Geneva set her fork on her plate. "That should have been good enough."

"But it wasn't. It couldn't be."

"She admitted to writing those checks." Geneva lifted her cup and sipped again. "That was poor judgment on her part."

"Dad was her employer," Dev pointed out. "She'd just completed a grueling year of night-school classes, taken after long hours of daytime work. She'd landed a dream of a job—for the most influential businessman in town—and she probably didn't want to do anything to jeopardize it. If she'd told her new boss she wasn't going to give him what he wanted, he probably would have fired her, and then she'd be out of work without a reference. What was she supposed to do?"

"The honest thing."

"Tell you what was going on?"

Geneva's expression hardened. "She could have, yes."

Dev shifted upright and forward. "Give me one good reason why she wouldn't do that."

"Why she wouldn't?" His grandmother was obviously surprised by the way he'd phrased his question, but then her brows puckered as she thought of a response. "She might not have been completely certain there was anything wrong with what Jonah was asking her to do."

"Do you buy that?"

Geneva hesitated, frowned. "No."

"Okay. Let's try another reason."

"Must we?" She poked her cooling omelet with her fork. "I'd like to finish my meal without this interrogation."

Dev shrugged and helped himself to another bite. They ate in silence for a few minutes, and then his grandmother brought her napkin to her lips, carefully folded it and laid it beside her plate. "Assuming she did think Jonah was doing something wrong," she said, "perhaps Lena was trying to protect him."

"From you?"

Geneva slowly nodded. "Perhaps."

"Why?"

Geneva's fingers pressed against the linen before she met Dev's gaze. "Because she suspected I knew your father was a failure."

"At business?"

"At everything."

Dev considered ending it there. After her protest, Geneva hadn't finished her meal. And in spite of her steely spined posture, he could see the signs of strain around her mouth. "Let's limit this to the problem of the missing money, shall we?"

"To Lena's problem?"

"To my father's."

"And what problem," Geneva said in a coldly precise tone, "are you referring to, exactly?"

"His gambling."

Dev had been watching her closely for a tell, and he didn't catch one. Not a twitch of her tightly pressed lips, not a deepening of the creases around her dark eyes, not a movement of her fingers on her napkin, not so much as a flicker of a lash.

Geneva was a woman in control of her emotions and appearance, but even she couldn't be that rock-steady. She hadn't known.

"What evidence do you have for that accusation?" she asked.

"I followed a hunch. Something Bud Soames mentioned at a poker game last week. It led me to his father, Win."

"Winston Soames."

"Yes."

Geneva dragged in a deep breath. "A gambling debt?"

"Yes."

"Not a failed business venture?"

"No. Although I discovered, while looking through his papers, that he wasn't doing well with those ventures, either."

"Oh, Jonah." She closed her eyes, and Dev wondered if she grieved again. "Did Lena know?" she asked.

"I'm not sure." He stood and paced to the window,

staring sightlessly at the limestone terrace brightened with flowers bursting from oversize concrete urns. "Which brings me back to an earlier question. Whether she knew or not, why didn't she come to you with her concerns? I thought you'd been close."

"We were. She may have been my housekeeper, but we were friends. Good friends. And I loved…I love her daughter as if she were my own."

"And yet you sent me to her." He turned to face his grandmother. "After all those years of warning me off, you practically threw me at Addie with that crazy window repair business and the lecture at the airport."

"Guilty as charged." Geneva picked up her coffee, sipped, grimaced, set it down.

"Why now?" Dev asked.

"I've thought for some time that you were ready to settle down and form a family of your own. I hoped you wouldn't hurt Addie this summer, and I took that chance. Besides, when I discovered she'd become involved with that nice young man, that ballplayer, and—"

Geneva smoothed her hand across her napkin with a sigh. "I'm so tired of waiting for my grandchildren to give me great-grandchildren. I can't wait forever."

"Back to Lena." Dev leaned against the window and crossed his arms, determined to see this through. "Why do you think she didn't come forward, earlier, with what she knew? Why didn't she put up a stronger defense?"

"I think she may have been trying to protect Jonah's reputation."

"Why would she do that, at the risk of losing her own?"

"She was in love with him."

Dev shut his eyes for a second. So many pieces fell into place with another of those silent clicks. "And yet he used her. Betrayed her. Set her up. No wonder she hates the Chandlers."

"Not all of us, surely."

Dev chuffed out a short laugh and shoved away from the window. "Don't kid yourself."

"I didn't press charges."

"If you had, she might have been able to clear her name."

"That's difficult to do in such a small town."

"No kidding." Dev slowly drew in a deep breath and blew it out. "Have you ever tried to make amends?"

"I wasn't the one writing those checks."

"So, you haven't forgiven her."

He was shocked to his core to see his grandmother's features collapse like softened wax and her lower lip quiver. The lapse in control lasted only a second, and then she raised her chin. "I want to make this right," she said.

"Then help me piece together the rest of this puzzle. Help me find out whether Lena wrote those checks for my father so that he could cover his gambling debts."

"All right." She fingered the edge of her napkin. "I'll talk to Winston."

"That's not all, I'm afraid." He shoved his hands into his pockets. You're going to have to grovel."

"I'll do it for you."

"I'm not asking you to."

His grandmother rallied with a smug smile. "If you continue seeing Addie, you'll reach that point soon enough."

"I've been told you suggested Jack Maguire start his

own business, and that perhaps Carnelian Cove might be a good location." Dev walked her and gripped the back of her chair. "And that you hired Quinn to be the contractor on Tess's project." He leaned down, his face close to her ear. "I don't think that even you could arrange for an earthquake to do your bidding, but I wonder if you took advantage of a natural disaster to use as a cover for the damage to those windows."

"That statue may have had a bit of assistance smashing into the glass."

Dev groaned and dropped into the chair beside her. *"Grandmother."*

"I'm an excellent matchmaker, if I do say so myself."

He shook his head. "You're as much of a gambler as my father was."

"I'm better." She raised one eyebrow. "And I play for higher stakes."

DEV PULLED TO THE CURB in front of A Slice of Light a few minutes ahead of schedule on Saturday night. He glanced in the mirror to check his tie and wondered whether he'd appear too eager if he knocked on Addie's door five minutes early. And then he figured he'd look like a fool if she saw him sitting here waiting, so he climbed out, grabbed his package and strolled to the shop door.

Everything mattered a great deal tonight. Though Addie wasn't yet aware of it, he was courting her. Officially.

There was something else Addie wasn't yet aware of. His steps slowed. When she found out he was investigating the mystery behind her mother's embezzlement scandal, she might put a stop to his courting before he had a chance to propose.

The scents of salt-washed docks and hot waffle cones sailed in from the bay, and the bass backbeat from a passing car's sound system thumped down the street. It all tangled with Dev's memories of summer evenings spent prowling the Cove's neighborhoods, a crowd of friends crammed into his rumbling muscle car. They may not have gone looking for trouble, but they'd found it often enough to keep the adults in their lives threatening curfews and doling out punishments.

The sign in Addie's shop window told him she'd closed early, and the knob he turned was locked. He cupped a hand against the glass and peered inside to see a single light glowing over the rear work area. The door to her apartment hung open, a dark gash in that long, curtained glass wall.

He lifted a hand, wondering if she'd hear his knock, and then he noticed a button set in the wall beside the lock. He pressed that and waited, shoving a hand in a pocket as more memories ghosted through his mind. Waiting like this in front of Sheila Gardner's front door on prom night, his tuxedo shoes pinching one toe. Cruising down the highway, Cyndi Mattison's floral perfume competing with the pine scent of his car deodorizer.

Addie opened her door and peered through the narrow crack. "Hi, Dev."

"Sorry, I'm early. I know that's the last thing a woman wants when she's getting ready for an evening."

"It's okay." She stepped back and beckoned him inside. "I'm nearly finished."

She shut and locked her door behind him. And when

she turned to face him, he froze, as tongue-tied as he'd been on his first date.

Smoke and mirrors, he thought as his eyes traveled over her. A mirage—it had to be. This woman wasn't the Addie he knew. And yet that was her hair caught up in twisting loops with sparkling pins, making his hands itch to pull them free and wrap those curls around his fingers. And those were her eyes, looking wider and bluer than ever and ringed with sooty, sexy smudges. And those were her lips, slicked with something that made them look as though she'd just run her tongue over them. And her bare shoulders and tiny waist, outlined in silver that glinted like stars. And her slender legs emerging beneath layers of gray froth, and oh, God, her bare feet. And her toes, with something shimmery on the nails. He made a mental note to pay special attention to those toes later, after the dance.

"Is that for me?" she asked, pointing to the tissue-wrapped bouquet he held at his side.

He tore his gaze from her toes and cleared his throat, extending the package toward her. "I brought you flowers. I thought you'd rather have them in a vase instead of on your wrist."

She looked puzzled for a moment, and then her cheeks dimpled as she gave him a dazzling smile. "A corsage. You didn't need to…I mean, thank you for the thought, but you—"

They stood, staring at each other, for several strange, awkward seconds while he doubted the wisdom of this date. He longed to sweep her into his arms and carry her into the special haven behind her bedroom screen, to keep her to himself. And then she took the flowers from his hand, and he relaxed enough to breathe properly.

"Come on back," she said. "I'll put these in water and get my shoes, and then we can go."

He followed her into her apartment and prowled through the front room while she filled a thick white pitcher with water. "I didn't get a chance to tell you the other night how much I like your things." He ran a hand along the edge of a scarred oak icebox. "They suit you."

"Most of them are thrift-shop finds." She placed the pitcher in the center of her table and fussed over one of the buds. "So they mostly coordinate with my decorating budget."

"Everything's unique." He stared at her legs as she dropped onto her love seat to slip on silvery sandals. "Like your windows."

She stood and brushed a hand over her skirt. "You're full of compliments tonight."

"You deserve them. Tonight."

"I suppose it's your turn." She tilted her head to one side. "I suppose I should tell you I like the scent of your aftershave."

"Yes, I think you should." He closed the distance between them. "Anything else?"

"I like your tie."

"I picked it out myself."

She looked up at him, smiling. "Did you pick out your shirt, too?"

"No. The salesman did that. He said it matched the tie."

"Yes, it does."

He started to lift a hand, to touch one of the glittery things in her hair, but let it drop. "Anything else?"

"I like the flowers you brought me."

"I thought so." He took her hand and led her toward her apartment door. "Anything else?"

"I like the fact that you were on time."

"I was early."

"Only a little," she said, lifting a tiny, sparkling handbag from her table as they passed. "But that meant I didn't have to wait for you."

"Any longer, anyway." He laced his fingers through hers. "I think we've both been waiting for this evening long enough."

CHAPTER EIGHTEEN

ADDIE CLUTCHED HER spangled bag as if it were a life-saver as Dev coasted beneath the porte cochere of The Breakers Golf and Country Club. She'd been too stunned by his invitation and too caught up in her friends' excitement to consider the impact of this moment. And now that the moment had arrived—as the valet opened her door and extended his hand to help her from the car—the stunning excitement had been replaced by fear.

She hadn't wanted to admit it, not even to herself, but there was no denying her apprehension about walking into Dev's world on his arm. She didn't need to hear the whispers as he led her through the tall entry doors—they hissed and echoed in her imagination, prickling the hairs at her nape. Isn't that Addie Sutton, the shopkeeper who lives in an alley? Wasn't she the housekeeper's daughter when Dev was in school? The daughter of the woman who embezzled all that money? Dev was always a wild one, but he's really slumming tonight, isn't he?

Dev rested his hand on her back as he guided her through the crowd gathered in the entry area. "Are you cold?" he asked with a frown.

"No. I'm fine, really." She gripped her bag more tightly.

"It's a perfect night." His expression transformed to an intimate, reassuring smile that warmed her a few degrees. "How about a drink?"

"Dev." A man who could have played Santa without the suit approached, his hand outstretched. "Good to see you."

"Samuel." Dev nodded as he pumped Samuel's hand. "It's been a long time. Have you met Addie Sutton, the owner of the stained-glass shop by the marina?"

"I haven't had the pleasure." The smile creases around Samuel's kind blue eyes made Addie feel as though he meant it.

"How do you do?" she said.

"I'm doing fine. Making the acquaintance of a beautiful young woman always makes me feel just fine." He reached for the arm of a woman handing a wrap to an attendant. "Martha, come and meet Addie."

"Addie?" Samuel's auburn-haired wife extended her hand. "What a pretty name."

"Stained glass, eh?" asked Samuel.

"She's an artist." Dev slipped an arm around her waist. "Wait 'til you see the windows she's making for that new building on the waterfront."

"Shame about the fire. That was shaping up to be a beautiful place…."

By the time Dev had maneuvered through the crowd to the bar, he'd introduced her to dozens of friendly people. More than one woman had complimented her on her dress—which was perfectly appropriate, thanks to Tess—and Addie's anxiety had eased so much that she ordered her usual glass of white wine instead of the stiff drink she'd been planning on.

But she kept her grip on her bag.

She managed to relax during dinner, enjoying the fabulous meal and reminiscing with Dev about favorite teachers and homecoming antics. But when the music started, her nerves returned. She stared at the couples gliding over the dance floor, moving in steps and patterns she didn't know.

"Amazing, aren't they?" Dev asked. "Those older couples will probably show the younger crowd a few smooth moves and stay later than anyone else."

Addie dropped her gaze to the napkin she was twisting in her lap. "Does everyone dance like that?"

"I think you have to be together a long time before you can dance like that."

"That's not what I meant. But you're right—it is amazing." She placed her elbow on the table and her chin in her hand, and then she jerked her hand back into her lap, remembering her manners.

Dev smiled and made a point of resting both his elbows on the table. He'd been doing little things like that all night, trying to put her at ease. He nodded toward the dancers. "Mel Franchi over there, twirling Stella around—I'll bet they've been dancing with each other for nearly fifty years. And they still look at each other like it's their first date."

"That's so sweet."

"They don't look a day older than they did the first time I saw them dancing like that," he said. "And that must have been twenty years ago."

"You probably thought everyone looked ancient." She finished the last of her wine. "I did when I was young."

"That would explain it."

They sat in silence through another tune, watching

as several more couples joined the crowd on the parquet floor.

"Looks like fun," Dev said as Mr. Franchi guided his wife through another fancy turn. "Let's give it a try."

"Oh, I don't know if I can." Addie squeezed the wrinkled napkin she'd laid on the table. "I don't know how to dance like that."

"We don't have to dance like that." He stood and held out a hand, waiting for her to take it. "We can make up our own steps."

"But I—"

"Come on, Addie. Just one dance. Just so we can say we gave it a shot."

She stared at his hand, wishing for a second that she'd never agreed to come here tonight. At last she slid her palm into his, and he gave her fingers a comforting squeeze as he helped her to her feet. He led her to a darkened corner, far from the band.

She stopped at the edge of the dance floor and tugged him close. "I really don't know how to dance like this."

He lowered his head, his mouth near her ear. "Trust me?"

"I'll have to."

"Come on, then."

He led her onto the floor, shifted his grip on her hand and placed his other hand low on her back. "We're just going to take a little walk," he told her, already moving. "All you have to do is move in time to the music and keep your toes out from under my shoes."

He kept it simple, one step after another, guiding her in a slow circle.

"Oh." She gave him a delighted smile. "We're doing it."

"Yes, we are." He grinned back, looking absurdly pleased with them both. "Ready for a trick? Let's shuffle off to the side."

Addie laughed, thrilled with the fact they were moving in sync. She tickled a finger along the back of his neck, and he drew her closer. And a few minutes later, when the music slowed and he rested his forehead against hers, she wondered whether they were as smooth and steady as the older couples surrounding them. It sure felt that way.

Dev was right. It was amazing.

"*Amazing,*" he whispered, in sync with her thoughts.

ADDIE COULDN'T HELP SMILING at her reflection in the long mirror above the counter in the ladies' room. Her hair was coiling madly and her lip gloss needed some serious repair, but the giddy delight ping-ponging inside her was on display, giving her a glow no cosmetics could hide. Tonight was making up for the disappointments of her prom experience. And several years of mediocre dinner dates. She hummed to herself as she leaned toward the glass to dab a bit of gloss on her lips.

"I saw you out on the dance floor, with Dev." Courtney Whitfield's reflection appeared beside Addie's. "He sure has some smooth moves, doesn't he?"

Addie managed an acknowledging smile and concentrated on the gloss.

"I remember him trying some on me, in cotillion.

That's ballroom dance class," she added for Addie's benefit.

"I know what it is."

"Looks like you were enjoying the benefit of all those lessons tonight."

"Yes."

"Better late than never."

"Addie Sutton. Is that really you?" Serena Bennett dropped her satin clutch purse on the counter beside Addie's. "I thought I saw you with Dev, but I couldn't believe it."

"Neither could I." Courtney smiled and shook her head. "It's amazing, isn't it? The heir to the family fortune dallying with the maid's daughter. Like something out of a novel."

"I think it's romantic." Serena stared at the mirror, finger-combing her short, highlighted layers.

"But then I remembered hearing old lady Chandler's been out of town." Courtney's smile sharpened. "When the cat's away…"

"Not all of them, at any rate." Addie dropped her gloss into her purse. "Excuse me, ladies. My date is waiting."

Addie's hands were shaking so badly as she walked out the door that she couldn't manage the clasp on the fancy little bag. She'd never been able to handle confrontation. She was glad she'd stood up for herself, but saying spiteful things always made her feel small and mean.

"Damn," she whispered.

DEV PACED THE WIDE passageway outside the ladies' lounge, waiting for Addie to reappear. She slipped through the door, shoulders hunched and chin down, fussing over the catch on her sparkly handbag.

"Here, let me help you with that." He gently pried the purse from her grip, frowning when he noticed her trembling fingers. "These things can be complicated."

"You have no idea." She took a deep breath and let it out slowly. "I'm sorry I took so long in there."

"The results were worth the wait." He returned her purse and took her by the arm, guiding her toward the entry. "I have something to tell you."

"What is it?"

He opened the door for her, and they stepped into a cooling summer evening. A layer of fog was moving in from offshore, bringing with it a briny ocean scent. He wondered if Addie might feel chilled in her sleeveless dress, and he slid an arm around her shoulders, drawing her to his side as he handed the valet his card.

"I took a call on my cell while you were in the lounge," he said after the valet had left to arrange for the car. "Tess has been trying to reach you. Your mother is in the hospital emergency room. She's doing fine now," Dev added immediately when she tensed and turned to face him. "But she'd like you to come as soon as you can."

"What happened?" Addie asked as the car arrived. The valet opened her door and stood waiting, but she ignored him. "Is she hurt?"

"No," Dev said. "She had some sort of attack."

"Her heart?"

"Tess didn't think so." He took her hand and helped her into the car, tipped the valet and jogged to the driver's side and slid in. "One of your mom's friends—"

"Laurie?"

"Tess didn't say." He pulled smoothly out of the lot, heading toward town. "This friend told Tess that one of the tenants in Lena's apartment building had gone to talk with her about a repair. He thought she was drunk, at first, because her speech was slurred and she seemed dizzy. But then he got worried when he noticed she couldn't move one of her arms, and he called an ambulance."

"Oh, God."

Dev grabbed Addie's hand and gave it a squeeze, wishing he could do more to ease her anxiety. "By the time the ambulance arrived, your mom was fine. Embarrassed by all the fuss. When she couldn't reach you, she called her friend, and the friend took her to the emergency room."

"And when my mom still couldn't reach me, she called Tess." Addie's fingers tightened on her little bag. "My phone wouldn't fit in this purse, so I left it at home."

Dev made a turn in the direction of Carnelian Cove General, keeping one eye on the road and another on the gauges. It wouldn't help matters if he were pulled over for speeding.

"How long has she been at the hospital? How long was she trying to reach me—did Tess say?"

"I don't know. We're on our way now." He rolled to a stop at a signal and flexed his fingers on the steering wheel. "You'll be there as soon as you possibly can."

"I shouldn't have left my phone at home."

"You couldn't have known you'd need it." The ragged pain and guilt in her voice was a knife, slicing deep, ripping him up inside. He started through the intersection, shifted into a higher gear and then reached for her hand again. "It's not your fault your mother is in the hospital. And it's not your fault you weren't there with her when she first arrived."

Addie's fingers curled around his, but there was no affection in the tiny embrace. She stared out the passenger-side window, and he sensed her slipping away, retreating behind the barrier her mother had always thrown up between them. He released her hand to adjust the car's thermostat and warm the space.

"What else did Tess say?"

"She made a point of letting me know Lena's doing fine." He gave Addie a reassuring smile. "She was feeling perfectly normal before she got to the emergency room. They're running a few tests. Just standard, routine tests."

"I'm sorry for ruining your evening."

"Apologizing again?" He downshifted around a corner and started up the long, steep approach to the hospital building. "That's a nasty habit you've got there, Addie."

He pulled into one of the spaces reserved for emergency room visitors and switched off the ignition. "And just for the record," he said, "the evening isn't over yet. You've got several more hours to do something more deserving of an apology."

She unbuckled her seat belt and grabbed the handle. "Thank you for bringing me here."

"You're welcome." He exited the car and strode to her side, but she'd already climbed out.

"You don't have to walk me in," she said as he took her by the arm and started down a path marked in diagonal white stripes.

"Like I said, the evening isn't over yet."

"You don't have to wait with me."

"I know."

"I can call a cab to get my mom home."

He tightened his grip on her arm. "When I invite a woman out for the evening, I see her to her door."

"What if you end up seeing her—and her mother— to her mother's door?" Addie asked as they arrived at the emergency entrance.

Dev opened the wide glass door and gestured for her to enter ahead of him. "There's a first time for every- thing."

CHAPTER NINETEEN

ADDIE'S DRESSY SANDALS clicked on the hospital floor and the chiffon floated around her knees as she followed the emergency department nurse toward her mother's curtained cubicle. How would she explain her fancy evening wear?

By telling the truth, of course. Part of the truth, anyway—just the part about tonight's date. And then she'd hope her mother wouldn't have a fit.

Another fit.

Good thing they were already in the hospital.

Addie pasted a smile on her face and smoothed an unsteady hand over her stomach as they neared the curtain.

The nurse pulled the drape to one side and entered first. "Still doing okay?" she asked Lena.

"As well as can be expected. *Addie.* Where were you? I—" Lena's gaze traveled from Addie's hair to her shoes and back again, her lips thinning in a tight frown. "Where have you been?" she asked as Addie leaned in to kiss her cheek. "I've been trying to reach you. Everyone's been trying to reach you."

"I was out on a date." Addie swept her mother's hair from her forehead and then let her hand fall to her shoulder. "I didn't have my phone with me."

"Why not?"

"It wouldn't fit in my bag." Addie moved it behind her back. She'd tried to be so stylish this evening, but carrying a shimmery purse wasn't worth the stress she'd added to Lena's evening.

"Excuse me." The nurse shifted in toward Lena's side and took her arm. "Let me get your blood pressure while I'm here."

Addie moved restlessly to the opposite side of the gurney and back again while the nurse checked her mother's pulse. Lena looked fine. A bit tired, a bit strained, perhaps, but that was to be expected. Her color was good and she didn't seem disoriented.

She seemed ready to give Addie a thorough grilling.

The nurse left, pulling the curtain closed behind her. Lena pointed to the chair. "Sit down."

Addie did as she was told. "What happened?" she asked. "What has the doctor told you?"

"I don't want to talk about that right now. I want to know where you've been."

"I told you." Addie slid her handbag into an empty space on the cart beside the gurney. "I was out on a date."

Lena's frown deepened. "It must have been some date, considering the way you're dressed. Where did you get those clothes?"

"Tess found the dress for me."

"It looks like something Tess would choose. And where was this date?"

"At The Breakers."

"The Breakers! How did Mick get into that place?"

Addie kept her gaze steady on her mother's. "I wasn't there with Mick."

Lena's eyes narrowed. "Please don't tell me you were there with Dev Chandler."

"How am I supposed to respond to that?" Addie stood and paced to the foot of the gurney.

"I warned you about that man."

"That was years ago. We were both much younger."

"Nothing has changed."

"I've changed." Addie pointed a finger at her heart. "And so has he."

She moved to her mother's side. "I like Dev. I like being with him. We're friends. I was thrilled when he asked me. I was having a wonderful time."

Lena turned her face toward the medical equipment dangling over the edges of a basket on the wall. "I'm sorry I spoiled it for you."

Filled with mortification and worry and guilt, Addie edged her hip over one side of the gurney and took Lena's hand. What was she doing? She was in an emergency room, arguing with a woman who might have had some sort of heart attack or stroke. A woman she loved, a woman who had always put her daughter first. "Mom. Don't."

"Don't what? Disapprove of a man who doesn't seem to care about anything but himself? Worry about my daughter spending time with him? You knew I would."

"Mom, please. Calm down. Lower your voice," Addie whispered. She took her mother's hand, needing the contact. "You shouldn't get yourself all worked up."

"Oh, *now* you think of how this news might affect me. Well, that's convenient. You obviously didn't consider my feelings before."

"Yes," Addie said, miserable and smothering beneath another layer of guilt. "I did."

"And yet that didn't stop you." Lena pulled her hand from Addie's and folded it with the other at her waist. "And what about Mick? What are you going to do when he finds out about this date?"

"Mick and I aren't seeing each other anymore."

"Oh, *Addie.*" Lena closed her eyes and shook her head, moving it from side to side against the pillow. "Since when? No, never mind. You don't need to answer that. Since Dev Chandler came back to town."

"It wasn't like that."

"What was it like, exactly?"

How could Addie explain that Mick had never lit her from within the way Dev could with a glance or a smile? How could she explain the miraculous night of lovemaking she and Dev had shared?

She pinched a fold, and then another, pleating the gray chiffon spread over her knees. The fabric seemed dull and lifeless in the harsh glare of the hospital lighting, insubstantial against the industrial-white sheet wrapped around the mattress. She felt alien in this place, in this skin, as though she'd been plucked from one world and identity and dropped into another.

None of it seemed to matter anymore. As she sat here with her mother, the memories of the past two weeks wavered and faded, losing their power to change her life. She felt herself fading, too, the color leaching from her. Soon she'd be as gray and transparent as the fabric of her dress.

"I broke up with Mick before Dev asked me to the dance."

"Because Dev is back in town, and you thought—you hoped—you could do better."

"I told you. Dev and I are friends."

"You were never good at telling a lie, Addie."

"It's not a lie. We are friends."

"Excuse me?" One of the clerks from the reception counter peeked through an opening in the curtain. "Addie Sutton?"

"Yes?" Addie stood.

"The gentleman out in the waiting room sent these things for you." She handed Addie a soft drink can and two women's magazines. "He asked me to remind you that he'll wait to give you a ride home."

"Please tell him thank you." Addie glanced at her mother. "And tell him that he can go now. We'll find some other way to get ourselves home."

DEV LOOSENED HIS TIE and slumped in one of the chrome-and-vinyl chairs in the emergency room waiting area. A seventies' car-chase scene careened in silent mayhem on the television screen suspended high in one corner. Across the room a toddler banged a dented toy car against the side of a plastic table while his mother browsed through a creased and faded travel magazine.

The dance floor at The Breakers seemed a world away.

And his memories of Lena seemed a lifetime ago. He hadn't been surprised, when he'd caught that glimpse of her at Addie's shop door, to see that she was still rail-thin, if she still pressed her lips together as though she could prevent one of her rare smiles from leaking too much happiness. He'd always thought that Lena believed joy was a finite commodity.

He glanced at his watch. A nurse had escorted Addie

into the treatment area nearly fifty minutes ago, and
there had been no word yet on her mother's status. Dev
considered whether if he could chance a search for
coffee without missing Addie if she came looking for
him. He supposed the receptionist could get a message
to her to ask if she'd like something more to drink, or
perhaps a snack—that is, if visitors were allowed to eat
in the treatment area.

As he stood, intending to check at the counter, Tess
strode through the wide door. "What are you doing
here?" he asked.

"Addie called and asked me to bring her a change
of clothes and something to read." Tess lifted a bulging
canvas bag. "She says she's very grateful for all your
help, but she may be here for several more hours.
You're free to go."

"Ordered to go, you mean."

"I refuse to get caught in the middle of this." Tess
shook her shaggy black bangs out of her eyes. "I'm just
the delivery girl."

Dev muttered a curse. "Lena probably threw
another fit when she found out where Addie had been
this evening. And with whom."

"You both knew she'd find out eventually, anyway.
Didn't stop you from going." Tess shrugged. "Don't
worry. You're too old to be grounded."

"I'm not leaving."

"Suit yourself." Tess shoved the bag into Dev's
arms. "Tell Addie I love her, and ask her to give me a
call when she gets a chance."

"Wait." Dev set the bag on the chair behind him.
"What's the number for the phone Addie used to call
you?"

"Clever," Tess said, "but that won't work. Cell phones are forbidden back there—too much interference with too many finicky machines. She called me from a pay phone down the hall."

She'd left her mother's side to use a pay phone, but Addie hadn't come to the waiting room to talk to him herself. Either she didn't want to see him, or Lena didn't want her to see him.

The fact that he couldn't guess which scenario was more likely made him more determined to stay and find out. Addie was going to have to talk to him—to deal with him—if she wanted her things. "Did she say anything else?"

"They've run a couple of tests, and there's one more to go. No one is saying anything for sure until they get the results, but the doctor who's been talking with them back there thinks Lena had a TIA. Transient something-or-other. Serious, but not life-threatening."

"Are they going to admit her?"

"Probably not. The fact that she snapped out of it so fast is supposedly a good sign."

"Thank God." Dev released a long sigh. He hadn't realized how tense he'd been, waiting and hoping to hear something positive. "Hard to imagine Lena in a hospital bed."

"She's a tough lady. I'm sure she'll be fine. Besides," Tess added, "she'll have Addie fussing over her."

The image warmed him clear through. "I'll bet no one fusses like Addie."

"Like mother, like daughter." Tess ran a finger along the edge of his lapel. "You look nice tonight."

"Thanks."

"Too bad things worked out the way they did." She flattened her palm over his chest and gave him an affectionate pat before dropping her arm to her side. "Okay. Gotta run."

"I'll make sure Addie gets her things."

The corners of Tess's mouth curled up in one of her catlike smiles. "I'm sure you will."

IT WAS NEARLY TWO O'CLOCK in the morning when Dr. Tripathi told Addie she could take her mother home. The initial tests indicated cholesterol was the culprit, but Lena's personal physician would schedule more tests, on an outpatient basis, during the coming week.

Addie thanked the emergency room doctor for his help and pulled the privacy curtain closed. Behind her, Lena swung her legs over the side of the gurney to step into her shoes. Addie lifted the extra sweater Tess had brought, waiting for her mother to slip an arm into one of the sleeves.

"I can dress myself," Lena snapped.

"Sorry." Addie handed her the sweater and backed away, already dreading the next battle. They were both exhausted and on edge. "Got your purse?"

"Right here." Lena pulled it from beneath the thin cotton blanket she'd shoved to the foot of the gurney. "We should call for a cab, although I'm not sure we can get one in this town at this time of night."

"We don't have to take a cab." Addie slung the straps of her canvas tote over one shoulder. "Dev is still waiting to give us a ride."

"We don't need his charity." Lena rummaged through her purse and pulled out a small compact.

"He knows that. But he chose to wait all this time

for us." And though he must have suspected his assistance wouldn't be welcome, he'd arranged for the receptionist to smuggle in candy and a deck of playing cards in addition to the drinks and magazines. "The least we can do is be gracious about accepting his help."

Lena didn't respond. But the way she freshened her lipstick and tugged a comb through her hair told Addie she was preparing herself for the inevitable.

"I thought I'd have Dev take us both to my place first," Addie said. "I need to get my truck. And then I want to spend the night at your apartment, so I can keep an eye on you."

"You heard the doctor. I'm fine, for now. There's no need for you to worry about me."

Addie rested a hand on Lena's arm. "I love you. I can't help but worry about you."

They walked together to the nurses' station, where they listened to a brief discharge lecture and Lena signed the paperwork. And then they moved through the wide double doors and into the noisy waiting area.

A young woman paced the room with a bouncing step, crooning to the squalling infant in her arms. In one corner, Dev sat in a plastic chair, hunched over a low table. Beside him, a pajamas-clad toddler ran a plastic truck over a stack of magazines, up Dev's sleeve and down again. The two of them growled silly truck sound effects.

Addie halted near the doorway, staring. She'd never imagined Dev interacting with a young child. Somehow he'd always seemed disconnected from the minor distractions and discomforts of everyday life, as though he'd never repaired a leaky sink or mowed a lawn or camped in a waiting room, tolerating the attentions of a little boy. "Dev."

He glanced over his shoulder and grinned. "Just a minute." After the truck rolled noisily off his arm, he murmured something to his playmate and then stood and stretched. "Good evening, ladies. Lena, it's nice to see you again."

"Hello, Dev." Her mother's back was so stiff and straight Addie wondered if it would crack when she moved. "Thank you for waiting."

"No problem." He pulled his car keys from his pocket. "Ready to go?"

Lena nodded, turned and headed toward the door.

"That's a yes, then." Dev jogged to the entrance to push the door open for her. "I'm parked in the emergency area, to your right."

He waited until Addie walked through and then fell into step beside her. "Your place?" he asked. "Or Lena's?"

"Mine. I'll get my car and take her home myself."

"Figured that might be the case."

He lengthened his stride, leaving Addie behind, and opened the passenger door for her mother.

Lena hesitated. "What kind of car is this?"

"A Maserati." Dev took her elbow and helped her inside. Addie caught a glimpse of her disapproving expression before he closed the door.

"It's a sedan," he told Addie as he guided her to the driver's side and reached for the handle on the back door. "A family car. Very suburban. All the Italian race car drivers' wives use these to haul their kids to soccer practice."

She smiled as she climbed awkwardly into the

backseat. Though there was much less leg room, the leather seats in the back still felt as though they'd cost a fortune.

"Addie says I'm taking you to her shop, so that's where we're going." He switched on the ignition and backed out of the spot. "Let me know if you'd like me to turn on the heat."

"I'm fine. Thank you." Lena turned her head toward her side window. End of conversation.

Dev glanced at Addie in his rearview mirror and gave her a sympathetic smile. She smiled back and settled against the cushiony seat, determined to endure her mother's silence without letting it tie her stomach in knots.

It felt so good to let someone else handle the driving for a change.

ADDIE AWOKE WITH A GROAN the following morning and shifted to her back, trying to find a more comfortable position. The sofa in her mother's living room wasn't the best place to spend the night, but she'd been too tired to care much where she slept, as long as it involved a horizontal surface.

A thump overhead told her Lena was up and out of bed. Addie slitted one eye open and checked the time on the cable box beneath the television. Seven o'clock. It appeared that four hours' sleep was all she was going to get.

She tugged the blanket under her chin and snuggled against the cushions, craving a few more minutes of drowsy warmth and relaxation before heading back to her shop and all the chores waiting for her there. Just a little while longer to float on memories of last night before facing the day—and her mother.

Dev had been so sweet last night. So patient, so kind. So different than what she'd expected. First dates were all about making a good first impression, but she and Dev were years past that point. Besides, they'd already shared an impromptu dinner. And spent the night together.

The fact that he'd tried so hard to make the evening special for her was endearing. Nearly suspicious. What was he up to?

She groaned again, upset with herself for searching for reasons to explain his behavior. What did it say about her, that she'd carried a torch all these years for a man she had believed was a terrible human being? That she'd looked forward to spending the evening with someone she'd once suspected might treat her badly? That she'd gone to bed with him?

The truth was far too complicated to understand without several more hours' sleep and at least one cup of coffee. Addie shoved off the sofa, folded the throw she'd used for a blanket and headed into the kitchen to start the coffeemaker.

A few minutes later Lena padded in on her fluffy slippers, wrapped in a pink robe and looking better than Addie felt. "I'll make you breakfast before you go."

"Thank you." Addie focused on the promise of food and ignored the invitation to leave. She opened her mouth to ask her mother how she was feeling but decided Lena was probably tired of hearing that question. "I was going to settle for a cup of coffee, but breakfast sounds great."

"All I have to offer is a bagel and fruit."

"I'll take it."

Lena sliced through the roll and dropped the two halves in her toaster. "Do you plan on seeing Dev again?"

"I'm sure I'll be seeing him often this summer, with Charlie's wedding, and all."

"That's not what I mean, and you know it." Lena turned to face her, leaned against the counter and folded her arms. "Are you thinking of becoming involved with him, socially?"

Socially. Addie frowned. She was in no hurry for a rerun of the scene in the ladies' lounge at The Breakers. But she'd survived the encounter with Courtney Whitfield. And dancing with Dev had been worth enduring all the uncomfortable moments of the evening.

Being with Dev was worth anything.

Except jeopardizing her mother's health. "He hasn't asked me," Addie told her.

"But if he does?"

"It depends, I suppose."

Lena turned away to deal with the food. She pulled a bowl of grapes and some cream cheese from the refrigerator, dropped the toasted bagel halves on a plate, grabbed a couple of paper napkins and set everything on the table. "Sit and get started. I'll get the coffee."

Addie slid into her chair, wishing she'd chosen a drive-through breakfast over this continuation of last night's argument. She didn't want to do anything more to upset her mother. She snapped a few grapes from their stem and popped one into her mouth.

Lena set a mug in front of her with an angry-sounding clunk and filled it with coffee. "You're making a big mistake, getting mixed up with Dev Chandler."

"I'm not mixed up with him."

"What do you know about him, anyway? He's never settled down. He probably never intends to." Lena sat and wrapped her hands around her own mug. "He has different values than you do."

"What can you possibly know about his life or his values?" Addie lifted her mug and blew on her coffee to cool it. "He's a grown man. He's not the same person he was ten years ago."

Lena spread cheese on her bagel. "Did you see that car?" she asked. "What kind of a car is that for a grown man with sensible values to drive? He probably paid more for that car than you make in goodness knows how many years."

"Is that what's troubling you? That Dev has money?" Addie set down her coffee. "That's not fair."

"It's not the money. It's how he chooses to spend it."

"If he promised to sell that car, would you be happy to hear that he'd asked me out again?"

"Don't put words in my mouth."

"Mom." Addie shoved her half of the bagel aside. She wouldn't be eating anything here this morning. And it seemed there was no way to avoid any unpleasantness. "I'm trying to understand why you have this prejudice against Dev. He's never done anything to harm you. And he was extremely kind last night. Kind to us both."

Lena pressed her lips together and shifted her gaze to the window.

Addie tried to think of something else to say, some way to break through her mother's irrational resentment, anything to get this discussion back on track. She twisted her mug in a tight circle on the table, feeling the familiar, gravitational pull of her mother's wishes suppressing her own desires, distorting their shape and meaning.

Sometimes pieces never fit together, and certain patterns never seemed to make sense. They simply existed.

WHEN DEV STEPPED THROUGH the door of A Slice of Light on Sunday afternoon, the look on Addie's face told him exactly how hard he'd have to fight to get things back where they belonged. He stopped at her counter, separated from her by the barrier. "How is she?" he asked.

"Fine."

"How are you?"

"Fine." Addie hid a yawn behind a hand and then touched her soldering iron to another spot on one of Geneva's windows. She wasn't wasting any time getting them finished.

"Fine enough to have dinner with me tonight?" he asked.

"I should take something over to my mother's."

"I could arrange for another takeout dinner." He leaned an elbow on her counter, hoping he looked more casual than he felt. "I think I'm a pretty good takeout cook."

"Yes, you are." She gave him a brief, wistful smile and then quickly glanced away. Too brief, too wistful. "I don't think that would be a good idea."

He wanted to leap over this barrier between them, to stalk into her work space and haul her into his arms and make her understand the real reason he'd come here today. He gripped the edge of the counter, his muscles bunching, but his feet stayed stuck in place. "Because your mother doesn't approve of me?"

"I don't know why she feels the way she does." Addie frowned and bent closer to her work. "You were very considerate last night."

"Damn it, Addie." He shoved away from the counter, searching for control of his temper. He'd never raised his voice to her, that he could remember, and he was ashamed he'd done it now. She was obviously exhausted and unhappy. "I wasn't being considerate. I was—"

Trying to prove his love? Trying to get into her mother's good graces? Taking care of her? Courting her? Which explanation would she want to hear? Which explanation could he bear to admit?

She lowered her head and scrubbed at a bit of glass. One of her clips slid to the side, and her hair draped softly over the back of her neck. "I didn't mean to make it sound like my mother and I are some kind of charity case."

"Good. Because I didn't mean it that way."

He watched her work for a few minutes, while a strained and miserable silence stretched between them. "Will you have dinner with me tomorrow night?"

"I'm waiting to see if my mother will be scheduled for any testing tomorrow. I'd like to go with her."

Medical testing that would likely be finished well before the dinner hour.

He'd give it one more try. Because it seemed, after

all, that he had no pride where Addie was concerned. "Will you have dinner with me any night this week?"

She slowly raised her eyes to his. Just for an instant, like the click of a camera shutter, he saw in her features a mirror of the same emotion that was coursing deep inside him. And then the shutter came down, and it was gone.

"No," she said.

ADDIE'S HEART BROKE a little when Dev sent get-well flowers to her mother on Monday. It broke a little more when he sent a bouquet of lemon-yellow daisies to her shop on Tuesday.

On Wednesday, Tess stopped by with coffee. Just for a prewedding check, she claimed. Just to make sure the bridesmaid dress was ready to go and that Addie was still planning on joining her friends for the salon appointment on the morning of the wedding. And by the way—did Addie know Dev was thinking of sticking around after summer? Geneva had mentioned he'd talked with her about a long-term stay in her guest house.

On Thursday, Charlie charged in at lunchtime, dropped into one of Addie's work stools and complained about the salon appointment. And had Addie heard that Dev was meeting with the chairman of the English department at the local university about a teaching job?

On Friday morning, Dev called while Addie was in the shower. He wanted to find out how Lena was doing, he said. And he had to check on the progress on the windows, because Geneva was nagging him about it. And he missed Addie, more than he could say on the stupid telephone to some stupid machine. She listened to the recording of his voice seven times before erasing his message.

CHAPTER TWENTY

ON FRIDAY AFTERNOON, Dev stalked into A Slice of Light and flipped the sign on the door to Closed.

"What are you doing?" Addie asked.

"Taking you to the wedding rehearsal."

"I don't have to leave for another two hours."

"We're taking the scenic route." He strode behind her counter, unplugged her soldering iron, grabbed her hand and dragged her toward her door. "I have something to tell you."

"Is it about my mother?"

"Yes."

"Oh, God."

"She's not sick." He waited while Addie locked her shop, and then he led her down the block to his car, opened the passenger side door and helped her in. "Not yet, anyway," he added.

"What is this about?" she asked as he pulled away from the curb. "Where are you really taking me?"

"To your mother's apartment."

"Why?"

"Because I want to go steady with you, but she's grounded you for life. I'm hoping we can negotiate better terms."

"You're talking nonsense."

"That's exactly what this feels like."

Addie stared out her side window while they made the trip across town, her fingers laced in a white-knuckled fist. "I missed you," she said at last.

"Same goes." He turned into Lena's apartment complex. "You got my message this morning, didn't you?"

"Yes." She twisted her hands in her lap. "I'm sorry I—"

"Don't apologize." He shot her a narrow-eyed glance. "Just tell me whether or not you erased the evidence of my incoherent babbling."

"I did."

"Okay, then." He nodded. "No apology necessary."

He pulled to a stop in one of the guest spaces near her mother's apartment and switched off the ignition. "Here's the deal. Geneva found out what happened to that money your mother supposedly embezzled all those years ago."

"How did—"

"I won't reveal my sources. Or my methods. I'll only admit that I put her up to it. And that I waited to tell you about this until I'd gathered all the facts." He glanced over Addie's shoulder at Lena's door. "I'm fed up with the enmity between the Suttons and the Chandlers. I'm not going to play Romeo to your Juliet. I'm ending this. Today."

He touched a hand to Addie's cheek. "Are you with me?"

"Yes."

"No matter what happens?"

She took his hand and gave it a squeeze.

"Okay, then." He started to open his door and then settled back against his seat. "One more thing."

"Yes?"

"I'm driving down to the city in a few days to get some more of my things."

"I heard you were moving back to the Cove."

"I want you to go with me. We can make a long weekend of it," he said with a flash of inspiration, "spend some time in the wine country." At a place with a whirlpool bathtub for two, he thought. And a shower that didn't run out of hot water before he'd finished with the soap.

"A vacation weekend?" She smiled. "I'd love to."

"And when we get back, I want you to move in with me."

Her smile faded.

"We'll talk about it later." He opened the door, jogged around to the passenger side and helped her out. "First we have to survive the next half hour."

DEV KNOCKED ON HER mother's door, and a few seconds later, Addie heard footsteps on the tiled entry floor inside. "What do you want?" Lena's voice was muffled through the door.

"To talk to you," Dev stated.

"I have nothing to say to you," came the answer.

"Mom." Addie knocked again. "Please. Let us in."

A few more seconds passed, and then the locks clicked open and Lena faced them, barring the path into her home. "What is this about?" she asked.

"We don't have a lot of time." Dev glanced pointedly at his watch. "Addie is due at Charlie's wedding rehearsal in another hour or so."

Addie didn't ever think she'd seen her mother

angrier—or more afraid—and the full force of her rage and distress was directed at her daughter.

Dev's hand closed around Addie's. She turned her wrist, slid her fingers through his and squeezed again. Choosing him. She took a deep breath and sidled past her mother, pulling Dev inside with her. "This won't take long," she said.

Lena followed them through her small apartment to the living room in the rear. Beyond the wide picture window framed with plain beige drapes, an elderly man walked his overweight bulldog and two young children played a noisy game of tag.

"What is this about?" Lena asked again as Dev took a seat beside Addie on the matching beige sofa. "Why are you here?"

"There is no easy way to start this conversation," Dev told her, "so I'll come straight to the point." He settled back against the cushion. "Why do you hate the Chandlers so much?"

Lena's gaze shifted to Addie. "You know why."

"No, I don't," Dev said, directing her attention back to him. "I've been told that my father turned off the audit trail on his bookkeeping software so he could take a certain sum of money without anyone being able to trace it. And that you were blamed for that after he died."

"Isn't that reason enough?" Lena began to pace through the room. "He set me up. I could have gone to prison. He stole my reputation. I lost any chance I might have had of working in a better-paying job in this town."

"He couldn't have known he was going to die that night. It wasn't a suicide." Dev's voice was calm, reasonable. "So he didn't set you up."

"He would have had to cover up the loss somehow.

He could have lied and blamed it on me. We were the only two people who knew the password."

"What about Geneva?" Dev shifted forward, his elbows on his knees. "She believed you. She dropped the charges."

"She never cleared my name."

"She was burying her son," Addie pointed out. "Dealing with her grief. To clear your name, she would have had to brand that son as a thief."

Lena turned on Addie. "So she branded me, instead."

"She kept you out of jail," Addie reminded her.

"She stole my future from me."

"I'm sure that if you'd gone to her," Dev said, "she would have written a reference for you."

Lena wrapped her arms around her middle.

Addie imagined the white-hot heat of her mother's anger would ripple the air around her like a desert mirage. "Mom. There's something you're not telling me. Something that's missing from all this. Some reason you hate Dev, too."

Her mother pressed her lips together in a stubborn line. Dev checked his watch. It was no good, Addie thought, her heart sinking. He'd tell her what he'd discovered, but she'd remain trapped in her resentment.

And Addie would have to choose between them, again.

Someone knocked on Lena's front door. "Excuse me," Dev said as he stood and exited the room. "That's for me."

"I saw the way he looked at you," Lena said when Dev had gone. "All those years ago, when you were too young to notice. He wanted you."

"I wanted him back." Addie fisted her hands over

her heart. "I still do. With every cell in my body, I want him. I want to be with him, to love him. I love him, Mom. And I feel like I'm dying a little inside every day having to choose between the two of you."

"You'll be sorry." Lena moved toward to the hall to check on Dev's whereabouts. "He'll use you and cast you aside like—"

"Like his father used you?" Queasy with a sudden rush of understanding, Addie pressed a hand to her stomach. "You were in love with Jonah Chandler," she whispered. "Did you—"

"No." Lena gulped and swallowed a choking sob. "He wouldn't have me."

"I'm sorry." Addie went to her mother and held her tight while Lena's body shook with violent sobs. "I'm so sorry."

Geneva stepped into the room behind Dev. "I beg your pardon for arriving at this little meeting so late. But I'm not going to ask anyone's forgiveness for accidentally overhearing the last few seconds of your private conversation."

Lena withdrew from Addie's embrace and moved to the window, her back to the others in the room.

"Lena." Geneva sank into a nearby chair and carefully arranged the pleats of her linen slacks. "I loved my son as much as you love your daughter. I loved him in spite of his faults—and he had many of them. One of his biggest faults was not loving you. Another was his selfishness. I know it brings you no comfort now, but he never would have made you happy."

"I would have made him happy." Lena whirled to face her former employer. "That might have made all the difference in the world to us both."

"I think you may be right. And that gives me more pain than you can imagine."

Addie was shocked to see Geneva's mouth tremble. The older woman clasped her hands tightly in her lap. "Jonah could have used more happiness in his life," Geneva continued after another few seconds of visible struggle. "I believe you would have brought that to him. But we'll never know that now."

She stood and moved to Lena's side. "I miss you, old friend. I could use more happiness in my life, too."

Addie's mother closed her eyes and leaned toward the window, resting her hands on the sill. She shook her head. "It's been a long time."

"And it will be difficult to move beyond the past. But I think it's worth the effort." Geneva glanced over her shoulder at Dev and Addie. "I think our families would appreciate the effort."

"I need more time." Lena straightened and inhaled a deep breath. "And I need to fix my face. I'm sure I must look a fright."

"May I wait here until you return?"

Lena nodded and stepped back. With her chin held high, she walked past Dev and Addie. "Excuse me," she said.

"Why are you still here?" Geneva asked Addie. "You have a wedding rehearsal to attend. I'll handle the rest of this."

ADDIE THOUGHT CHARLIE'S all-white wedding was the most beautiful celebration she'd ever seen. Everything was perfect—the weather, the setting, the flowers, the food, the handsome groom and his well-behaved bride. Even watching Quinn solemnly mop

Tess's crumpled, red-nosed, tear-streaked face had a certain charm.

Her mother had decided against attending, but Addie was certain she'd come to Tess's wedding. There were too many years of pain to overcome in such a short while, but Lena was made of tough stuff. Addie hoped she'd inherited some of that backbone.

She shifted in her chair at one of the tables near the dance floor, craning her neck, looking for Dev. He'd been prowling the edges of the crowd at the reception, sending her scorching glances that promised another passion-filled evening of playful caresses, drenching pleasure and fiery lovemaking. Addie shivered, thinking of what he could do to her in the meantime with his affectionate squeezes and sweet kisses. A complicated man with a simple way of showing her how he felt.

"Looking for someone?" Dev dropped into the chair beside her, a plate of all-white cake in his hand.

"Looking for you," she said.

"Looks like you found me." He gave her his most wicked smile. "I have something to tell you."

"Oh, no."

"Yeah. Brace yourself."

He forked up a piece of cake, popped it into his mouth and chewed. "You know," he said after he'd swallowed, "not so very long ago, someone told me that if you can find a way to make a living doing the thing that makes you happy, you'll have a happy life." He took another bite of cake. "I didn't need to find a way to make my living because everything I needed was simply handed to me. And maybe, because of that, I got lost for a while trying to find the one thing that would make me happy. But I finally figured out what that one thing is."

He stopped for another bite. Addie's heart had started drumming a hard, insistent beat when he'd begun his speech, and she thought it might burst if he didn't continue. "What?" she asked, her voice a raspy whisper.

"Loving you." He shrugged and dug into the cake. "I've always loved you, you know."

"That's nice to hear." She tugged the fork out of his hand and shoved the plate out of his reach. "I've always loved you, too."

"I figured. You were just too stubborn to admit it."

"Maybe I was waiting for you to say it first."

He lifted her hand to his mouth and grazed her knuckles with his lips, staring at her with hot, dark eyes. Stealing her breath with that searing gaze, with that same fierce yearning she'd seen on his face in their high school parking lot so many years agao. With that same intensity she'd felt when they'd met again at the kitchen door and when they'd sat in the echoing stairway, and when he'd brought her ice cream on a summer afternoon. And when he'd moved inside her for the first time and made them one. "Why are you always so tough on me?"

"Do you want me to apologize?"

"No. I want you to marry me."

Oh, Dev. Dev, Dev. "Don't we have to go steady first?"

"No, let's skip straight to the engagement. We have to make up for lost time."

"We could elope."

He shook his head. "Geneva would kill us both."

"I don't suppose my mother would be too happy with us, either."

"God," he said, wincing. "You know, they're going to have to work together on the wedding plans."

"That's a happy thing to do together."

He frowned, obviously unconvinced. "If you say so."

And then he stood and tugged her from her chair. "Dance, with me, Addie. Let's get in plenty of practice, so we can be one of those amazing couples who move together like they've been doing it forever."

She let her hand rest within the warm, solid weight of his for a few moments, and then she gave it a little squeeze. "I thought you'd never ask."

Bestselling author Lynne Graham is back with a fabulous new trilogy!

PREGNANT BRIDES

Three ordinary girls—naive, but also honest and plucky…

Three fabulously wealthy, impossibly handsome and very ruthless men…

When opposites attract and passion leads to pregnancy… it can only mean marriage!

Available next month from Harlequin Presents®: the first installment

DESERT PRINCE, BRIDE OF INNOCENCE

* * *

'THIS EVENING I'm flying to New York for two weeks,' Jasim imparted with a casualness that made her heart sink like a stone. 'That's why I had you brought here. I own this apartment and you'll be comfortable here while I'm abroad.'

'I can afford my own accommodation although I may not need it for long. I'll have another job by the time you get back—'

Jasim released a slightly harsh laugh. 'There's no need for you to look for another position. How would I ever see you? Don't you understand what I'm offering you?'

Elinor stood very still. 'No, I must be incredibly thick because I haven't quite worked out yet what you're offering me.…'

His charismatic smile slashed his lean dark visage. 'Naturally, I want to take care of you.…'

HPEX0110A

'No, thanks.' Elinor forced a smile and mentally willed him not to demean her with some sordid proposition. 'The only man who will ever take *care* of me with my agreement will be my husband. I'm willing to wait for you to come back but I'm not willing to be kept by you. I'm a very independent woman and what I give, I give freely.'

Jasim frowned. 'You make it all sound so serious.'

'What happened between us last night left pure chaos in its wake. Right now, I don't know whether I'm on my head or my heels. I'll stay for a while because I have nowhere else to go in the short term. So maybe it's good that you'll be away for a while.'

Jasim pulled out his wallet to extract a card. 'My private number,' he told her, presenting her with it as though it was a precious gift, which indeed it was. Many women would have done just about anything to gain access to that direct hotline to him, but his staff guarded his privacy with scrupulous care.

Before he could close the wallet, his blood ran cold in his veins. How could he have made such a serious oversight? What if he had got her pregnant? He knew that an unplanned pregnancy would engulf his life like an avalanche, crush his freedom and suffocate him. He barely stilled a shudder at the threat of such an outcome and thought how ironic it was that what his older brother had longed and prayed for to secure the line to the throne should strike Jasim as an absolute disaster.…

* * *

What will proud Prince Jasim do if Elinor is expecting his royal baby? Perhaps an arranged marriage is the only solution! But will Elinor agree? Find out in DESERT PRINCE, BRIDE OF INNOCENCE by Lynne Graham [#2884], available from Harlequin Presents® in January 2010.

HARLEQUIN *Presents*

Bestselling Harlequin Presents author

Lynne Graham

brings you an exciting new miniseries:

PREGNANT BRIDES

Inexperienced and expecting, they're forced to marry

Collect them all:

DESERT PRINCE, BRIDE OF INNOCENCE
January 2010

RUTHLESS MAGNATE, CONVENIENT WIFE
February 2010

GREEK TYCOON, INEXPERIENCED MISTRESS
March 2010

HARLEQUIN® *Blaze*™

New Year, New Man!

For the perfect New Year's punch,
blend the following:

- *One woman determined to find her inner vixen*
- *A notorious—and notoriously hot!—playboy*
- *A provocative New Year's Eve bash*
- *An impulsive kiss that leads to a night of*
  explosive passion!

When the clock hits midnight Claire Daniels
kisses the guy standing closest to her, but
the kiss doesn't end after the bells stop ringing….

Look for

Moonstruck

by *USA TODAY* bestselling author

JULIE KENNER

Available January

red-hot reads

REQUEST YOUR FREE BOOKS!

2 FREE NOVELS PLUS 2 FREE GIFTS!

HARLEQUIN®

Super Romance®

Exciting, emotional, unexpected!

YES! Please send me 2 FREE Harlequin® Superromance® novels and my 2 FREE gifts (gifts are worth about $10). After receiving them, if I don't wish to receive any more books, I can return the shipping statement marked "cancel." If I don't cancel, I will receive 6 brand-new novels every month and be billed just $4.69 per book in the U.S. or $5.24 per book in Canada. That's a savings of close to 15% off the cover price! It's quite a bargain! Shipping and handling is just 50¢ per book*. I understand that accepting the 2 free books and gifts places me under no obligation to buy anything. I can always return a shipment and cancel at any time. Even if I never buy another book from Harlequin, the two free books and gifts are mine to keep forever.

135 HDN EYLG   336 HDN EYLS

Name	(PLEASE PRINT)	
Address		Apt. #
City	State/Prov.	Zip/Postal Code

Signature (if under 18, a parent or guardian must sign)

Mail to the **Harlequin Reader Service:**
IN U.S.A.: P.O. Box 1867, Buffalo, NY 14240-1867
IN CANADA: P.O. Box 609, Fort Erie, Ontario L2A 5X3

Not valid to current subscribers of Harlequin Superromance books.

Are you a current subscriber of Harlequin Superromance books and want to receive the larger-print edition?
Call 1-800-873-8635 today!

* Terms and prices subject to change without notice. Prices do not include applicable taxes. Sales tax applicable in N.Y. Canadian residents will be charged applicable provincial taxes and GST. Offer not valid in Quebec. This offer is limited to one order per household. All orders subject to approval. Credit or debit balances in a customer's account(s) may be offset by any other outstanding balance owed by or to the customer. Please allow 4 to 6 weeks for delivery. Offer available while quantities last.

Your Privacy: Harlequin is committed to protecting your privacy. Our Privacy Policy is available online at www.eHarlequin.com or upon request from the Reader Service. From time to time we make our lists of customers available to reputable third parties who may have a product or service of interest to you. If you would prefer we not share your name and address, please check here. ☐

HSR09R

COMING NEXT MONTH

Available January 12, 2010

#1608 AN UNLIKELY SETUP • Margaret Watson
Going Back
Maddie swore she'd never return to Otter's Tail...except she *has* to, to sell the pub bequeathed her, and pay off her debt. Over his dead body, Quinn Murphy tells her. Sigh. If only the sexy ex-cop *would* roll over and play dead.

#1609 HER SURPRISE HERO • Abby Gaines
Those Merritt Girls
They say the cure for a nervous breakdown is a dose of small-town justice. But peaceful quiet is not what temp judge Cynthia Merritt gets when the townspeople of Stonewall Hollow—led by single-dad rancher Ethan Granger—overrule her!

#1610 SKYLAR'S OUTLAW • Linda Warren
The Belles of Texas
Skylar Belle doesn't want Cooper Yates around her daughter. She knows about her ranch foreman's prison record—and treats him like the outlaw he is. Yet when Skylar's child is in danger, she discovers Cooper is the only man she can trust.

#1611 PERFECT PARTNERS? • C.J. Carmichael
The Fox & Fisher Detective Agency
Disillusioned with police work, Lindsay Fox left the NYPD to start her own detective agency. Now business is so good, she needs to hire another investigator. Unfortunately, the only qualified applicant is the one man she can't work with—her ex-partner, Nathan Fisher.

#1612 THE FATHER FOR HER SON • Cindi Myers
Suddenly a Parent
Last time Marlee Britton saw Troy Denton, they were planning their wedding. Then he vanished, leaving her abandoned and pregnant. Now he's returned...and he wants to see his son. Letting Troy back in her life might be the hardest thing she's done.

#1613 FALLING FOR THE TEACHER • Tracy Kelleher
When was Ben Brown last in a classroom? Now his son has enrolled them in a course, so he's giving it his all, encouraged by their instructor, Katarina Zemanova. Love and trust don't come easily, but the lessons yield top marks, especially when they include falling for her!

HSRCNMBPA1209